SPECIAL AGENTS
FULL THROTTLE

Also in the SPECIAL AGENTS *series:*

1 Deep End
2 Final Shot
3 Countdown
4 Kiss & Kill

Coming Soon:

SPECIAL AGENTS

6 Meltdown

SPECIAL AGENTS

FULL THROTTLE

sam hutton

With special thanks to Allan Frewin Jones

Thanks also to Paul Clift-Lands, Colin Robinson
and Jules Langley

HarperCollins *Children's Books*

First published in Great Britain by HarperCollins *Children's Books* 2005
HarperCollins *Children's Books* is an imprint of HarperCollins*Publishers* Ltd
77-85 Fulham Palace Road, Hammersmith, London W6 8JB

The HarperCollins *Children's Books* website address is
www.harpercollinschildrensbooks.co.uk

1 3 5 7 9 8 6 4 2

ISBN 0 00 714846 1

Chapter illustrations by Tim Stevens

Printed and bound in England by Clays Ltd, St Ives plc

Prologue

Holland Park.

London, W11.

Late August.

A blood-red Jaguar XKR Coupe raced through the winding streets, its low-slung body hugging the ground, its broad, alloy wheels gripping the road tightly.

It was six thirty in the morning. Spike Marshall was at the wheel: nineteen years old, pumped full of adrenaline and ready to go.

"Next left," shouted Billy Salter. He was at Spike's side – using a map he'd found in the glove box to navigate.

The Jaguar bumped up the kerb as Spike spun the wheel.

"Come on – let's make some sparks!"

"Yeah, let's see how fast she can really go!"

The two back-seat passengers screamed encouragement as Spike gunned the engine.

The four teenagers were on a mission. They were about to make some money.

"Second right!" Billy shouted above the pounding stereo blasting out Xfm at full volume.

The car lurched across the road. No signals. No warning. Spike laughed loudly – he felt invincible behind the wheel of a car, pushing seventy at times in the empty streets. Nothing could touch him.

"There it is!" Billy shouted.

They were in a mews terrace. Billy was pointing at a particular car – a yellow Bentley Continental T.

Spike slammed on the brakes and brought the Jaguar to a halt on the opposite side of the street.

The four young men stared across at the Bentley.

"Sweet!" Spike said, getting out of the Jaguar.

The others watched him intently as he strolled across the road to the other car. Spike ran his hand over the Bentley's immaculate bonnet, smiling. The stainless-steel radiator grill glinted in the early light. He stooped and peered in through the window. The seats had a dark leather trim. The dash was machine-tooled aluminium. There was a racing-car steering wheel.

Spike took his time, letting his fingers trail over the smooth, polished metal as he circled the car. He came to the driver's door and casually tried the handle, at the same time scanning the fronts of the mews houses. The door was locked. He glanced at his watch, then hoisted himself up on to the Bentley's bonnet, one foot on the wing, the other hanging down nonchalantly while he waited.

⊗

Meanwhile, a perfectly ordinary man walked briskly towards the mews terrace. He was wearing a dark Gieves & Hawkes suit. A crisp, white T.M.Lewin shirt. A neatly knotted Thomas Pink tie. He was carrying a silver metal briefcase. He checked the street sign and looked at the map displayed on his mobile communicator.

Excellent. He was almost at the target zone.

As he turned into the terrace, he saw a young man sitting on the bonnet of a yellow Bentley. Jeans. T-shirt. Cropped hair.

The man stepped back, out of sight, and waited.

⊗

Robert Fraser stood in the hallway of his home, checking his reflection one last time before leaving. He

was in his early forties, a typical businessman in a dark blue suit. He folded the *Financial Times* under his arm and picked up a black briefcase.

Before he made his way to his office in Whitehall, he was stopping off somewhere – private business. A few details to go over. It wouldn't take long.

He opened his front door and saw someone sitting on the bonnet of his car.

Shock and anger flooded through him. He dropped his briefcase and ran towards the car. "Get off there!" he shouted. "What do you think you're doing?"

"Hello, Bobby," Spike said with an evil grin. "How's business?"

Fraser halted, gasping, staring. "You!"

Spike jumped down off the bonnet of the car. His fist came out like a piston. There was no warning. Just the body blow.

Fraser doubled up. He slumped down on to the pavement, staring up at the grinning Spike.

Three more faces appeared. Fraser knew what was coming. He curled in on himself, his arms up to protect his head as blows and kicks rained down on him.

⊗

"OK," Spike panted, drawing back from the huddled shape. "That's enough. Mick – Tony – you take the Jag.

Me and Billy will finish up here."

Spike crouched over the still shape, slipped off Fraser's Rolex and gold signet rings, then pulled the Dunhill wallet from Fraser's trouser pocket, along with a bunch of keys. He carefully removed the car key from the bunch and dropped the others on the prostrate body. "Let's go," he said.

Billy pointed towards the house. The door hung open. "He'll have some good stuff in there," he panted, running up the path.

"No!" Spike called, looking around. They had been lucky so far – but someone might appear at any moment. "Time's up."

Billy halted in the doorway, staring back at Spike. He spotted the fallen briefcase. He snatched it up and ran back to the Bentley.

Spike was in the driving seat.

The Jaguar drove off with a roar from the other side of the street.

Billy jumped into the passenger seat of the Bentley as Spike revved up.

The turbo-charged engine gave a deep-throated throb. Spike hit the accelerator and the car lunged forwards. He knew the performance he could expect from this car: zero to 90 kph in 5.7 seconds. Grinning, he pursued the Jaguar down the road, wondering if he could get ninety-five out of her before he caught them up.

Within seconds, both cars were gone. Stillness descended on the quiet mews.

⊗

The man with the silver briefcase had watched all this without a flicker of expression on his face. As soon as the two cars had sped off, he stepped from cover and walked over to where Robert Fraser lay.

He knelt at his side. "It's OK," he said. "They've gone."

Gently, he turned the man on to his back. Fraser was still conscious. Badly beaten – bruised and bleeding from a cut lip. One eye was swollen and already closing. There was a gash along his forehead.

Fraser squinted up at the man bending over him.

The face swam into focus. "George?" Fraser whispered.

"It's been a long time, Bob," said the man. He smiled. Then he helped Fraser to his feet and guided him up the path and into the house.

Fraser leant heavily on him, his feet stumbling, his body wracked with pain.

"Let's get you sorted out, Bob," the man said. "That's a nasty cut you have on your forehead."

"Upstairs," Fraser gasped. "The bathroom. I need to clean up."

George guided Fraser up the stairs. He could hardly walk.

"You don't want to get blood all over your carpet," George said as they went through the living room. "It's a Sanderson weave, isn't it? Very nice. I have one just like it."

Fraser didn't respond.

Another flight of stairs led them to the bathroom.

Fraser leant heavily over the basin and turned on the tap. Blood dripped into the swirling water that he splashed over his face.

He straightened up and looked into the mirror. George had come up to his side. His face was totally devoid of emotion as he held a gun to the side of Fraser's head.

Fraser was too stunned to do anything other than to stare at the reflection of the gun.

"Sorry, Bob," George said. "The General is very upset with you."

⊗

George replaced the gun in his silver briefcase. He took a pair of black kid gloves out and slowly drew them over his hands.

He leant over the body and turned off the taps in the basin.

He stepped back and snapped the briefcase shut.

He picked it up and walked on to the landing. He went down the stairs.

He picked up the phone and pressed out a three-digit number.

He picked a thread off his jacket as he waited for a connection.

"Hello. Yes. Police, please."

He looked around the living room while he waited to be connected. It really was a very nice place. Was that a Picasso on the wall?

"Police?" he said. "Yes. Thank you. I want to report a murder."

Chapter One

Maddie Cooper gripped the steering wheel as the Vauxhall Vectra raced towards the wire fence. Her head was thrust forwards, her eyes fixed on the road ahead. The tension was like a ball of iron in her stomach.

Paul Dane's voice barked out. "Sharp left here. Now!"

Maddie didn't even glance at the man beside her – it was all down to her. She needed every ounce of concentration and focus. She fought down the panic that threatened to overwhelm her as she pressed down hard on the brake and turned the wheel.

"Too slow!" Dane shouted. "If they catch us we're dead meat!"

A long, narrow stretch of road lay ahead.

A car appeared – out of nowhere – sideways on to her – blocking the road.

"J-turn! Now!" Dane shouted.

Maddie slammed on the brakes. She was thrown forwards as the car slewed to a halt.

Two men in black overalls raced towards the car. They wore ski masks. Maddie was aware of long dark shapes in their hands. Weapons of some kind.

Maddie grasped the gear lever and thrust the car into reverse.

"Get us out of here, Agent Cooper! Now!" Dane shouted.

A gunshot cracked.

Maddie twisted in her seat, trying to keep the car straight as it sped backwards along the road. She had been trained in this manoeuvre – but the stress of the situation clouded her mind.

Think! Reverse at speed. Halt. Get the car under control. Turn the car around. Escape!

Sweat ran down Maddie's face as she wrenched the wheel around. The two men were gaining. She had only moments before they would be on her. She gunned the engine. She shook as another shot rang through the air.

The car swooped across the road in a tight turn. She

put her foot on the gas. The car leapt forwards.

"That was too close," said Dane, staring over his shoulder. The men were falling rapidly behind.

"What now?" Maddie gasped. She was trembling. She could taste the bitterness of adrenaline in her mouth.

"Straight ahead. It isn't over yet. They're not going to give up that easily."

Maddie blinked the stinging sweat out of her eyes. The blood pounded through her temples.

Two cars emerged on the edges of her vision – one from the right – one from the left – converging – cutting off the line of her retreat.

"Ram them," Dane shouted.

"I can't!" Maddie cried.

"Do it! Do you want to die out here?"

The two cars filled Maddie's vision – bumper to bumper. The drivers had got out. They were also in black. Masked. Pointing weapons.

Maddie aimed at the narrow gap between the two cars and floored the accelerator. Her fingers dug into the steering wheel. She narrowed her eyes – bracing for impact.

She hit the cars dead centre. There was a huge bang – the screech of beaten metal – the force of impact. But she was through! The two cars had been hammered aside.

The sudden release of tension caused her to give a short laugh. She was home free.

"Bear right!" shouted Dane. "We're not out of trouble yet."

She sped along a narrow road. The tarmac ahead of her was flooded. She came to a bend and felt the wheels slipping away beneath her.

"Keep your speed up!" screamed Dane. "They're right on our tail."

Maddie increased their speed, struggling to keep a straight line on the slippery road surface.

The road curved. The surface kept changing. Tarmac – asphalt – concrete. She couldn't control the car.

A shape loomed straight ahead. A young woman. Standing in the road – frozen – staring with shock.

"You're going to hit her!" shouted Dane.

Maddie kicked down hard on the brake pedal. The wheels locked. The steering was gone. The car skidded forwards, turning slightly, but heading straight for the woman.

Maddie tried to remember her training.

Cadence braking: Foot off the brake. Regain steering for a moment. Steer away from the woman.

Foot on brake. Reduce speed. Foot off brake. Steer clear. Foot on again. Bring the car to a controlled stop.

That was what her brain was telling her to do – but her body wouldn't obey. She was skidding at terrible speed towards the young woman. Every instinct told her to keep her foot on the brake. She couldn't help herself. The car careered onwards. Maddie tried to compensate for her mistake. She pushed down on the gas.

The car leapt forwards.

"Off gas!" shouted Paul Dane. "Maddie!"

The road whirled in front of her eyes. She had lost it. It was over.

She gave a gasp of relief as she passed to the left of the woman. Then she saw the low wall.

They hit the wall hard – a glancing blow that tipped the car on to its side.

Maddie clung on grimly as she felt the world flip over and over.

There was a deafening screeching noise – violent movement – disorientation and chaos.

Then the shuddering and the screeching stopped. The car had slid to a halt on its roof.

Maddie hung upside down in her seat belt, her eyes wide with shock. Her ears were full of the sound of the protesting engine. She was still clinging to the steering wheel, panting with shock.

It had all gone wrong so very quickly.

She was vaguely aware of Paul Dane leaning across her and switching off the ignition. He kicked his door open and crawled out. He made no attempt to help her.

Maddie was breathing hard and fast, her brain scrambled. She loosened her seat belt, crumpling down on to the car roof.

She twisted around, reaching for the door handle, and managed to prize the door open with her feet. She crawled out on to the wet road. Holding the car for support she staggered to her feet. Dizzy. Hurting.

Paul Dane was standing on the other side of the car. "You OK?" he asked.

"I think so," Maddie gasped.

"You were doing fine until the pan," he said.

Maddie stared out over the concave disc of the Hendon Driving School skidpan. It was shaped like a shallow wok. There were different road surfaces. Jets sprayed water. In places a slick of silicone gel lay on the surface. Over to her left was the open area where ramming training was undertaken as part of the Anti-hijack Course. This was the last day. The big test.

In the distance, she could see the running track and the accommodation-block towers.

She had been sent here as part of her on-going Police Investigation Command training. Despite the fact that Maddie was the youngest of the fast-track trainees, DCS Jack Cooper wasn't prepared to let her off lightly – even though she was his daughter.

"I can't believe I messed up like that," said Maddie. Anger and frustration were taking the place of shock. "I've failed the whole thing!"

"It's not a question of passing or failing, Agent Cooper," said Dane. "It's a question of knowing what to do in an emergency situation." He looked at her. "Now you know what to do. And what not to do."

Maddie's eyes blazed. She was so angry with herself. "I'll get it right next time," she said.

A new voice intruded.

"Interesting parking."

Maddie looked round. Alex Cox was walking towards them. He was a fellow PIC trainee, three years older than Maddie. An east Londoner, cherry-picked from Hendon by Jack Cooper for his elite team.

Maddie looked at her instructor. "I'd like a second chance," she said.

Dane lifted an eyebrow.

"Not today, Maddie," Alex said. "I've had a call from the boss. He wants us back at Control. Now."

Maddie gave Paul Dane a determined look. "This isn't over," she said. "I'll be back."

Dane nodded. "Sure, I'll be here. Anytime."

Maddie and Alex walked side by side away from the upended car.

"So," Alex said with a mischievous smile, "will that affect your no claims bonus?"

⊗

Whitechapel Road, London, E1.

The Blind Beggar Pub.

The pub was busy with lunchtime drinkers. Danny Bell made his way through the crowd. Locals. A few office types. Tourists, eager to see the pub where the Kray brothers had held court in the 1960s. The Krays had been gangsters – not unlike the men who had run his hometown of Chicago way back in the 1920s. Danny and his father had only been living in the UK for the last twelve months. The young black American was another of Jack Cooper's fast-track trainees. A great field agent and an electronics genius.

Danny was looking for one of his informants. He ran a whole network of people – petty crooks on the fringes of the criminal world. Sometimes they came up with the goods, sometimes they were a waste of time and money. It was always a gamble.

Fly was sitting in a corner, huddled over two glasses – a pint of beer and a whisky chaser. He was thin and nervy with sharp, black eyes and oily hair. Danny had always assumed he was in his late twenties, although he had the wasted, drug-abused look of someone twice that age.

Danny straddled a chair on the other side of the small round table.

Fly stared at him. "You're late," he whispered. His eyes were darting about all the time.

"So sue me," Danny said. "What have you got for me, Mr Fly?"

Fly leant close. Danny pulled away from his sour breath. "Hot stuff, Mr Bell," he said. "It's worth half a ton."

"Fifty pounds?" Danny laughed. "Goodbye, Fly." He made as if to get up.

"A pony, then," said Fly. "It's worth a pony to you, Mr Bell. A measly twenty-five quid."

"Keep talking," said Danny.

"I've been doing some manual labour over in Deptford," muttered Fly, his eyes darting every which way. "A bit of loading and unloading in a warehouse – know what I mean?"

Danny nodded. Anything Fly was involved in had to be illegal.

"It weren't the usual stuff," Fly continued. "Not fags nor drugs nor nothin' like that. It was these big wooden crates, right?" He wiped his hand across his nose and took a swig of whisky. Danny eyed him patiently. "Anyway, I started to wonder what's going on. Heavy great crates, they was. About twenty of them. They had 'Agricultural Machinery' stencilled on the sides, but I knew it weren't no farm gear. No way. So I broke one open just to have a quick shuftie inside. D'you know what I found?" Fly's eyes widened and he leant even closer. "Guns, Mr Bell. Big guns." He spread his arms wide. "Like army guns. Rocket guns and stuff like that. Heavy artillery."

Danny's eyebrows rose. "Have you been on the sauce, Fly?" he said, nodding towards the half-empty beer glass in front of the skinny man.

"No way. Honest to God, Mr Bell. I was stone-cold sober." His eyes became sly. "The thing is, them crates are being shipped out of the country in a few days. I don't know when, exactly. But it ain't going to be long, Mr Bell." His eyes glinted. "I knew you'd be interested. Soon as I saw them big guns, I thought to myself, Mr Bell will be interested in this. Oh, yes."

Danny looked at the man. He had no intention of

letting Fly know exactly how excited he was by what he had just been told, but it was difficult to suppress the thrill that was racing through him. This could be just the break that he had been hoping for.

"I might check it out," Danny said coolly. He took out his wallet and peeled off a note. "Here's twenty," he said. "Spend it wisely, Fly."

A claw-like hand shot out and the money vanished. Fly dropped a grubby scrap of paper on the table. Danny picked it up. It had an address scrawled on it. He folded it in half and slipped it into his pocket.

Danny stood up. He leant close over the man. "You tell anyone else about this and I'll ask Mr Cox to make a call on you, get the picture?"

Fly nodded. He knew Alex Cox. A dangerous young man. He had no intention of getting on the wrong side of him.

As soon as he was out of the pub, Danny let a grin break across his face. He ran to where the car was waiting. Gina was at the wheel.

"Any good?" she asked as he climbed in.

"You'd better believe it," Danny said. "I've just been given some info that could bust Operation Golden Fleece wide open." He laughed. "Control, Gina. And step on it."

Chapter Two

PIC Control.

Briefing Room.

13:45.

DCS Jack Cooper sat in his wheelchair at the front of the room. He was in his fifties, a grim, taciturn man with iron-grey hair and piercing eyes. The gangland assassination attempt that had robbed him of the use of his legs had done nothing to blunt the keen edge of his mind. Police Investigation Command was his baby – he ran the whole show from his penthouse office in the Centrepoint building.

There were about twenty agents in the room, each with their own computer terminal – two department heads, field agents, Control staff and three fast-track trainees: Maddie, Danny and Alex.

Tara Moon stood by the door. She was Jack Cooper's personal assistant – twenty-five with short red hair and steely green eyes. Not a woman to be messed with.

Outside the door, the red light was on – Briefing In Progress. No Entry.

"Item one," said Jack Cooper. He glanced at Danny. "I believe Mr Bell finally has something to tell us on Operation Golden Fleece."

Maddie brought the background file up on her screen and skimmed quickly through it – refreshing her memory. This was not one of the cases she was working on, but she had read the files before. DCS Cooper insisted that all his staff have a broad understanding of everything that went on at Control.

Operation Golden Fleece.

International Arms Smuggling.

Military weapons from many NATO countries are getting into the hands of terrorist organisations. Evidence built up over a period of months suggests strongly that there is a single organisation behind this illegal trade – a smuggling cartel that refers to itself by the code name 'Hydra'. PIC is conducting an on-going investigation into the UK arm of this organisation in liaison with Europol and the central law-enforcement agencies of other NATO countries.

Danny came up to the podium.

He pressed a button on a remote control. An aerial map appeared on the large screen at his back. He picked up a pointer.

"OK, this is a bird's-eye view of Deptford, South London," he said. He pointed to a loop of the Thames. "Greenwich Reach." A railway line. "Deptford Station." A road. "Creek Road, SE8." He worked his keyboard and the map zoomed in close. He tapped the pointer. "If Fly is telling me the truth, then this warehouse is full of heavy artillery, packed in crates and marked up as agricultural machinery."

"What kind of weapons are they?" Alex asked.

"Fly said they were big," Danny replied. "He said they looked like army guns." He leant on the podium. "One thing's for sure – they shouldn't be there. I think we've found one of Hydra's nests." He looked at Jack Cooper. "My recommendation is that we get over there with the MSU and stake the place out at a discreet distance. If we go in heavy, we'll net the small fry but the big fish will get away. And what we need now are some big fish. We need to be able to make a direct link right up to the guy who runs Hydra in this country.

"I agree," said Jack Cooper. "I want a permanent PIC presence in Deptford – twenty-four hours a day. Danny, this was your lead so I'm putting you in control of the field operation. Keep a low profile – back off if you think they suspect anything. You have a watching brief – await developments. Keep in permanent contact. Don't make a move without referring back directly to me, or to Section Head Susan Baxendale if I'm not available."

Danny left the podium.

"Moving on," said Jack Cooper. "Item two. This is a new case for us – Operation Hubcap."

Maddie and the others clicked on the file.

"Something from the boys at the Met," said Alex.

It was headed:

Metropolitan Police – Serious Crimes Squad.
Stolen Vehicle Unit – SO7.

This unit has been undertaking an operation against a London-based gang involved in top-of-the-range organised vehicle theft. The scale of this car ring means that it is beyond the scope of borough-based police units.

"OK," said Jack Cooper. "The story behind this is that a big car ring has been up and running for several years without SO7 getting anywhere near to breaking it. The Home Secretary has recommended to the Serious Crimes Squad that they pass the case on to us at PIC." He gave a wry smile. "The Home Secretary believes that our special expertise may help to create a long-awaited breakthrough." He scanned his agents. "I believe the Home Secretary is correct in thinking that. Now, let me show you the kind of vehicles that SO7 believe are being targeted."

He typed on the keyboard. "You'll note that they are all high-performance, very expensive, luxury vehicles."

The wall screen showed a rapidly changing series of photographs of cars. Jack Cooper named them as each picture appeared.

"BMW 5 series. BMW 7 series – especially popular right now. Ferrari 328 GTS. 550 Marnello. F355 FI Berlinetta. F355 Spider. Mondial 3.2 Cabriolet. Bentley Arnage. Bentley Continental. Mulliner. Azure. Keep up with me – there's more. Lamborghini 350 GTS. Miura P400SV. Espada series 1, 2 and 3. Jarama S. Urraco P300. Rolls Royce Corniche. Rolls Royce Park Ward. Rolls Royce Silver Seraph. Porsche 911. Porsche Boxer."

"This is big money," Danny said under his breath. "There must be some rich guys at the top of this business."

"PIC's remit," Jack Cooper continued, "is to infiltrate this ring. To find out how it runs and who is running it."

Maddie felt a shiver of anticipation and excitement as her father's eyes turned towards her.

"Agents Cooper and Cox are assigned as undercover operatives for this case," said Jack Cooper. "I want to see them in my office in ten minutes. This briefing is over. Back to work, everyone."

Maddie stared at Alex. She could hardly believe it – a few minutes ago she had been expecting to spend the rest of the day at her work station in Control, and now she was about to go undercover for the first time since joining PIC.

"Some guys get all the breaks," Danny said with a grin. "I'm going to be in Deptford for the next few days, squatting in the back of the MSU and hoping something interesting happens, and you two guys will be strutting around town stealing Rollers and Ferraris."

Chapter Three

Alex and Maddie stood in front of Jack Cooper's desk.

The boss of PIC was giving his daughter a long, thoughtful look. "This is your first official time undercover, Maddie," he said. "Alex has more experience than you, so consider yourself under his command for the duration of the operation."

Maddie nodded. No problem. She had absolute faith in Alex.

"Tara has drawn up a plausible background for the two of you," Jack Cooper continued. "Listen and learn."

Tara was standing at the side of Jack Cooper's desk. "I've kept it simple," she told them. "You're both from

Southend. Maddie Brown and Alex Smith." She looked at Maddie. "We're using your real first names to keep it simple on your first undercover mission."

Tara consulted her notebook. "You've known each other for several years," she continued. "You've been involved in petty theft – shoplifting and so on – but neither of you have criminal records. That would be too easy for a suspicious person to check on. You both left home over a year ago." She gave a slight smile. "You fell out with your parents big time and haven't been in touch with them since you left. You were living in a squat. You came to London to make some money. You've been here for two months now, sleeping rough when you couldn't get into hostels or squats. For the past few weeks you've been living in a hostel in Battersea – that will explain why you're not street-filthy."

"What clothes should we wear?" Maddie asked.

"There's some appropriate gear in Supply," said Tara. "Choose things that will fit the character profile."

"Are we an item?" Alex asked.

"No," Tara said. "Good friends, that's all. You do your thieving together. You're a team. We don't want it to look like Maddie is just disposable eye candy. Part of your job is to make sure you don't get separated." She snapped the notebook closed. "Work out the rest of the details between you. And make sure you always tell the same story."

Alex and Maddie looked at one another.

"We already have one good lead," Jack Cooper told them. "A lad was picked up at the wheel of a stolen Porsche two days ago." He opened a Manila folder and took out a DVD in a clear plastic envelope. "This is a recording of his interview," he told them. "I haven't seen it, but I'm told that he said things that strongly suggest he's linked to the car ring. Take a close look at it and then report back to me."

The interview.

The boy was in his late teens. He was dressed in smart, casual clothes, trying to look cool – but his eyes were glancing nervously towards the camera. His voice was low and hesitant.

"I don't know anything about any car ring," he said. "I just saw the car and I thought I'd like to take a ride, know what I mean?"

"In a Porsche?" said the interviewing officer. "Come on, Jake, the sooner you tell us the truth, the sooner you can be out of here. Who asked you to steal the car?"

Jake glowered for a few moments, obviously thinking hard. "I don't know the bloke's name," he muttered. "I don't know anything."

"Of course you do, Jake," said the police officer. "Make it easy on yourself. Where were you told to leave the Porsche?"

Jake eyed the officer. "Apex Carwash – King's Cross Arches."

"That's more like it," said the officer. "Now – who's your contact there?"

"I don't know him," Jake admitted. "I never met him. He calls me when he's got work for me, right? He gives me an address and a make of car. I go to the place and I steal the car. There's a drop-zone. I drive it into a bay behind Apex Carwash. I don't see anyone. The bloke leaves 500 pounds under a paving stone. I take it." A smile spread over Jake's face. "I spend it. I wait for bloke to call again. That's all I know."

"You've never met the man?"

"No."

"How did you first make contact with him?"

"I was in The Moon and Sixpence pub in Stepney. I got chatting to some bloke about cars and stuff. He told me how I could make some easy money. I had to give him my mobile number. I was told another bloke would call me." He shrugged. "That's how it works. I get my instructions over the phone. I do the deed. I take the money."

"So, you have no idea what happens to the cars after you drop them off at King's Cross Arches?" asked the police officer.

Jake shook his head. "Don't know, don't care."

The interview continued for another half an hour or so while the police officer tried unsuccessfully to prize more information out of him.

It seemed unlikely that he was keeping anything back.

He was just a foot soldier. Strictly cash-in-hand.

⊗

Alex touched a key and the screen went blank. "Five hundred quid a car," he said. "Nice work if you can get it." He looked at Maddie. "Jake is our role model for this operation. Do you think you can act like that?"

Maddie fixed Alex with a cold, deadly stare. "You got a problem with the way I act?" she said, her voice a low, hard snarl.

Alex stared at her, surprised by how quickly she had changed character. "Back off, girl," he said. "I'm not picking an argument with you."

"You'd better not." Maddie's icy expression

softened and she laughed. "I'll get into it even better once I'm in costume. How are we going to play this?"

"We could take a trip over to The Moon and Sixpence in Stepney," Alex said. "Put ourselves about a bit – ask some questions. Let people know we're a couple of idiots looking for fast cash."

"Or we could take a car out of the police car pool," Maddie suggested. "Drive it over to King's Cross Arches and see what happens."

Alex smiled. "The direct route. Yes, I like that." He stood up. "Let's go and get kitted out – then we'll report to the boss and see what he says."

⊗

Maddie and Alex reported to Jack Cooper's office. The clothes they had picked up from Supply were shabby but clean. Old jeans. T-shirts. Rumpled jackets. Rough old trainers. Maddie had loaded her hair with gel and had scraped it back hard and flat. Astonishment flickered for an instant in her father's eyes as she came slouching into his office. He wasn't used to his daughter looking like a street thug.

He listened closely to Alex and Maddie as they briefed him on Jake's interview. Then Maddie made her pitch for taking a car direct to King's Cross Arches.

"What do you think?" Jack Cooper asked Alex.

"It makes sense to me," Alex said.

Jack Cooper nodded. "OK. Do it." He looked at Maddie. "How did you get on at Hendon?" he asked.

"Fine," she said guardedly. "I'd like to go back some time and work on a few details."

Alex said nothing.

Jack Cooper's expression didn't change. "Like learning to park with the wheels downwards, you mean?"

Maddie's shoulders slumped. He'd already heard of the disaster on the skidpan. "I'll get it right next time," she said.

"I know you will," said Jack Cooper. His eyes became very sharp. "You realise that you are under no circumstances whatsoever to get behind the wheel of a car during this operation? Alex will do all the driving." He looked at Alex. "Is that understood?"

Alex nodded. "Yes, boss."

"Once you're undercover, I want you to make contact at regular intervals," Jack Cooper said. "Don't take any unnecessary risks. Don't underestimate the people you'll be dealing with. Use your brains – if you find yourself in trouble, call for backup before it's too late."

He opened a drawer and took out two slimline mobile phones and two small black devices.

Alex recognised one of the devices – small enough to slip into a pocket, it was an electronic car alarm disabler. Point – press a button – and virtually any car alarm on the market would turn itself off. Alex had used one before. A very handy gadget to have around.

"I want you to take these phones," Jack Cooper said. "They're the smallest models we could find."

He handed the second of the black devices to Maddie. It looked like a mini-calculator. "This is a telephone decoder," he explained. "Tara will instruct you on its use before you leave. Keep these things out of sight," he went on. "If there's any danger of them being found on you – dump them. But try not to lose the phones. Keep them on you at all times. They may be your only lifeline if you get in trouble."

Cooper looked closely at Maddie. She got the feeling her father was debating whether to say something extra to her. The moment passed.

"I'm agreeing your plan," he said briskly. "Speak with Tara – she'll give you clearance to take a car out. I have complete confidence in both of you. Dismissed."

Chapter Four

King's Cross Arches, N1.

17:55.

Alex and Maddie sat in the midnight-blue Rover 45. They had been there for thirty-seven minutes. The Apex Carwash was closed and shuttered. The back alley was of rough gravel. The high, dark wall of the railway arches reared to one side. There had been no activity since Alex had driven the car in here at eighteen minutes past five.

Following Alex's lead, Maddie had pushed her new mobile phone down inside her sock. She was very aware of it – pressing against her ankle – but at least it would be safe down there. The decoder was tucked into the other sock. "How long do we wait?" she asked.

"A couple of hours, minimum," Alex replied. "If nothing happens by then, maybe we should switch to Plan B – go pay a visit to The Moon and Sixpence."

Maddie frowned. "Let's try to get some action here before we do that," she said. She leant across the car, switching the ignition on. She rammed the heel of her hand down on the horn. Once. Twice. A third, long, blaring blast.

Alex looked at her.

She half-smiled at him. "I'm a bad girl in a hurry to get rich. I'm not sitting around all day, waiting for someone to pay attention to me. I'm making some noise."

"Job done," said Alex. He pointed. A gate had opened a crack in one of the arches further along the viaduct. A man stood there, staring at them. Alex opened the door and climbed out of the car. He leant on the roof, staring back at the man.

The man began to walk towards them. He was wearing stained overalls. He wiped his hands on a rag as he approached. Thickset. Heavy features. Cropped hair. In his forties.

Maddie got out of the car.

"You want something?" the man called.

Alex walked up to him. Maddie was only one step behind.

"I've heard there's work," Alex said.

The man frowned, looking him up and down. "What work?"

Alex gestured towards the Rover. "Work for people who are good with cars."

The man looked at the car and shook his head. "I don't know what you're talking about, sonny," he said.

He turned as if to go.

Alex caught his arm, stopping him.

The man stared at Alex's hand.

Alex withdrew it. "I was told to come here," he said. "I was told there were people who would pay me five hundred pounds if I brought a hot car here. Come on – you know what I'm talking about."

The man eyed Alex with hostile suspicion. "Where'd you hear a crazy thing like that?" he asked.

"The Moon and Sixpence in Stepney," Alex replied.

"Sorry, sonny," said the man. "I can't help you. You've got your wires crossed."

Maddie stepped forward. "Stop playing games with us," she said, her voice hard and uncompromising. She looked at the car, and then glared at him. "The Rover's just to show you we can deliver. Tell us a make of car you want, and we'll get it for you." He held her eyes for a few moments, then looked at Alex.

"What have you got to lose?" Alex asked. "Let us in on the deal and we'll throw the Rover in for free. What do you say?"

"I don't need Rovers," said the man, shaking his head. "I can't help you. And if this car is stolen, I want it out of here, now!" He turned.

Maddie glanced at Alex. It seemed like they had blown it.

The man looked over his shoulder. "Of course, there is a car you *could* look out for," he smiled. "A black Special Edition Freelander Xei. *That's* a car I'd like to see."

He walked back to the gate and closed it behind him.

Alex and Maddie looked at one another.

"You heard the man," Alex said. "Let's go find a Freelander."

⊗

The London Eye.

23:45.

The Thames was a long silver snake, way below the glass and steel pod of the gigantic, endlessly revolving wheel. The buildings were lit up all along the Embankment. City towers were fretted with points of light. The sky was black.

There were only three people in the pod.

Jack Cooper. Tara Moon. And one other.

She was Christina Brookmier. A first division government employee. Power-dressed. In her fifties. Her dark hair drawn back off her pale, angular face.

Jack Cooper had known her for over twenty years. She had been in the SAS in the old days. An injury had forced her to move from active duty. She had joined the Ministry of Defence, rising rapidly through the administrative ranks. She now held a prominent position in the Defence Procurement Agency. She was one of the six members of the Executive Board, answerable only to the Chief of Defence Procurement.

It was more than five years since Jack had seen her. A phone call out of the blue had brought him and his PA to this specially arranged meeting on the London Eye. She said she needed to talk to him in complete confidence.

But as the pod lifted into the night sky, she seemed reluctant to talk.

"What can I do for you, Chris?" Jack Cooper asked, breaking the long silence.

Christina Brookmier turned from staring out at the spectacular night-time panorama. The expression on her face suggested she had not simply been admiring the view.

"I take it you've been keeping up with the news, Jack," she said. "You'll already know about the murder of a member of my staff – a man named Robert Fraser."

Jack nodded. "Found dead in the bathroom of his mews terrace on the 24th," he said, reciting from memory. "His personal possessions were gone, his car was missing, but the house was untouched. The police received a 999 call. The caller said he had to report a murder. The phone line was left open. The call was traced. The caller was gone. Robert Fraser was found dead with a single bullet wound to the head." He looked enquiringly at Christina. "He worked as a senior advisor to the Executive Board of the Defence Procurement Agency. In fact, I believe he worked directly for you, Chris."

"That's correct," said Christina. "As you know, our main premises are in Abbey Wood in Bristol, but we also have several offices in Whitehall. Fraser worked in London most of the time." She frowned. "For reasons I'll come to later, I've been based mainly in Whitehall for the past few months. I got to know Fraser quite well." She looked at Jack Cooper. "The Serious Crime Squad are investigating the murder, but there are aspects of this case that I'm not prepared to discuss with SO1."

"And that's where PIC comes in, I presume," said Jack.

Christina nodded. "I've been running an internal investigation," she said. "We've been concerned for some time that there was a mole at work in the Agency – someone relatively high-up – who has been acting as the UK head of the arms smuggling organisation that calls itself Hydra."

Operation Golden Fleece was hunting for information on Hydra UK – but how was the international arms smuggling cartel linked to the death of a Ministry of Defence civil servant? "There's no mention of an internal investigation on any of the files I've seen," said Jack.

"We don't let everyone see our dirty linen, Jack," Christina said with a tight smile. "And I'm trusting you to keep this strictly confidential." She glanced at Tara. Jack Cooper's PA gave her a stony look. Christina Brookmier nodded, as if to show she trusted them both.

"You suspected Fraser of being involved with Hydra?" Jack asked.

"We were close to completing the investigation," Christina explained. "Fraser was our prime suspect. We had already learnt a lot of curious facts about him. For instance, he had a lifestyle that far outstripped his income. He had no other legitimate source of money that we were able to find – which meant he was subsidising his spending from a hidden source."

"What specific evidence do you have?" asked Jack.

Christina looked at him. "Nothing incriminating so far," she said. She moved closer to him. "But here's the thing, Jack. I think he got wind of the investigation and planned to skip the country before we could pull him in." She leant in tight. "I believe he made contact with someone high-up in Hydra and told them he was under investigation. He probably asked them to help him get out of the country. I think they decided to kill him rather than risk him being arrested."

"If that's the case, then the theft of his personal belongings and of the car was just a blind," Jack mused. "You're looking for a paid assassin – perhaps from overseas."

"No, not quite," said Christina. "What I'm looking for – what I want PIC to look for – is Fraser's briefcase. SO1 cordoned off his home and his office as soon as news of the murder got through. They've searched both places. His briefcase hasn't been found, Jack. Nor has any kind of personal diary or organiser. Fraser had to have a list of contacts – codes, addresses. I'm guessing they were in the briefcase." Her eyes glinted. "I need to have that information, Jack. If we can lay our hands on it, we could close down the whole of the UK arm of Hydra. Without it, they'll just set up a new UK chief and we'll have to start from scratch. Months of work will have been wasted and Hydra will still be able to function."

"What makes you think the information you're looking for still exists?" Jack asked. "The assassin would have been told to destroy it."

"There's good reason to believe that the briefcase was stolen from Fraser before the assassin arrived," replied Christina. "The SO1 forensic team's report suggests that Fraser was beaten up and robbed before he was shot. And an eyewitness has two young men driving Fraser's Bentley at high speed along Holland Park Avenue at exactly the same time as the police were receiving the call about the murder. Bloodstains on the pavement outside Fraser's house suggest he was beaten to the ground there. His house keys were found in the gutter – as if they'd been kicked out of the way after the robber had removed his car keys. The SO1 team believe Fraser was beaten up and robbed outside his house by a gang of young thugs. They took his wallet, his briefcase and his car keys. Fraser dragged himself into the house. While he was in the bathroom, the assassin caught up with him. End of story." She put her hand on Jack Cooper's arm. "No one knows that we were investigating Fraser, Jack. I want it to stay that way. That's why I've come to you – as a friend – to do what you can to get that briefcase back."

Jack looked at her. "I'll do what I can, Chris."

She smiled.

As they talked, the pod had been moving slowly down to ground level. The doors opened. Tara wheeled Jack Cooper out. Christina Brookmier shook hands with him.

She melted away into the night.

Jack Cooper seemed deep in thought. Tara didn't speak until they were in the car.

"Why didn't you tell her about Operation Golden Fleece, sir?" she asked.

Jack Cooper looked at her. "The MoD have their secrets," he said. "And so do we. I don't hand over information concerning on-going PIC operations to outsiders."

"Is she an outsider, then, sir?" Tara asked as she started the car.

Jack Cooper smiled grimly. "Everyone not on the team is an outsider, Tara. You know that."

"Yes, sir. Where to now, sir?"

"Take me home, Tara. I want all the files on Operation Golden Fleece on my desk first thing in the morning. And I want you to make contact with the Serious Crime Group – I want to see everything that SO1 have on the murder of Robert Fraser."

Chapter Five

Saturday.

PIC Control.

Maddie felt apprehensive and excited as she and Alex left the Briefing Room and made their way to the lift. If things worked out, this would be their last visit to Control for a few days. From now on, they had to immerse themselves in their roles. There would be no clocking-off and going home. Once they had made firm contact with the criminals they would have to be Maddie Brown and Alex Smith of Southend twenty-four hours a day until the operation was complete.

Alex and Maddie had come into Control to brief

Jack Cooper on their progress so far. They had come up with a plan for laying their hands on a Freelander. He'd approved it. Now they had to put the plan into operation.

Jack Cooper had distributed a file to all personnel on duty that morning. Top secret. The file outlined his discussion with Christina Brookmier and asked that all field agents be alert for anything that might lead to the recovery of Robert Fraser's property. The file was given Priority Orange. Second-degree priority. Jack Cooper was not prepared to throw all his resources into the search until he was satisfied that it was a worthwhile use of manpower.

Alex and Maddie weren't using Alex's motorbike to get around – it would raise too many questions for a couple of street punks to be seen with a gleaming and well-maintained Ducati.

Maddie stared up at the Centrepoint tower as they walked out into the street. She felt like she was stepping out of the world she knew and understood and taking a blind leap into the unknown.

She was glad she had Alex with her.

⊗

Used-car dealer Jonathan Ainsley stepped out of his office. He frowned as he drew his Burberry jacket on and walked quickly and determinedly between the sleek, shining shapes of a BMW M3 Convertible and a four-door Bentley Arnage.

He had seen the two ill-dressed teenagers peering in through the windows of his Park Lane showrooms. His suspicions had turned to irritation when they had come inside. His Mayfair dealership traded exclusively in top of the range models. Those two looked as if they'd have trouble scraping together enough money for the tube fare to Marble Arch.

Jonathan Ainsley was used to dealing with time wasters. He quite enjoyed it. Politely but firmly, he would get them off the premises or he would telephone the police and have them forcibly removed.

A supercilious smile played over his face as he confronted them beside his latest acquisition, a Special Edition Freelander Xei.

Alex looked at him, disliking him instantly.

"Don't tell me," Jonathan Ainsley said. "You're eccentric millionaires and you'd like to pay cash. Am I right?"

"Not quite," Maddie replied mildly. "We're police officers and we'd like to borrow this vehicle for a day or two."

"If that's OK with you," Alex added, smiling politely.

Jonathan Ainsley laughed. This was a new one on him. Police officers!

Alex drew out his PIC ID card and held it up in front of Jonathan Ainsley's face.

"That's very good," the salesman said. "Except that I've never heard of PIC, and I wouldn't let you drive out of here in one of my cars even if you had a signed letter from the Prime Minister." A grin spread over his face. He stared out past Maddie and Alex. "I've got it," he said. "This is one of those TV shows, isn't it? Where you play practical jokes on people." He looked at Maddie. "Don't I know you from television?" He smiled broadly. "Sorry, but I'm not playing along. Nice try, though."

Maddie and Alex looked at one another. Maddie glanced at the name tag attached to the salesman's breast pocket.

"Please listen very carefully to me, Mr Ainsley," she said. "This isn't a TV show. We are police officers and we need to requisition this vehicle. I'd like you to go into your office, call directory enquiries and ask for the phone number of the Home Office in Queen Anne's Gate. Once you get through to the switchboard, please ask for the Home Secretary's Office."

Jonathan Ainsley stared at her. She didn't look crazy, but it was hard to tell. He decided that it was best to go along with them for the moment. If things got out of hand, he could always call the police.

They followed him to his office. He picked up the phone and did as they had asked.

Eventually, a crisp, polite voice answered. "Home Secretary's Office. Linda Jennings speaking. How may I help you?"

"Just a moment, please." Jonathan held the phone out towards Alex and Maddie.

Maddie took it. "Could you give me security clearance, please?" She heard a click as the on-line security protocol was put in to operation. She pressed out an eight-digit number, then Linda Jennings' voice came on again. "Security clearance complete," she said.

"Could you put me through to the Home Secretary, please?" Maddie said.

Jonathan Ainsley's eyes widened.

Maddie handed him the phone. "Tell the Home Secretary who we are and what we want to do," she said.

Jonathan Ainsley took the phone from her. This was turning out to be a very strange day.

⊗

Alex drove the black Freelander along Euston Road. Maddie sat at his side. They were still laughing about the look on Jonathan Ainsley's face as he had handed over the keys.

The Home Secretary had cleared the operation and had promised that the Home Office would cover any damage or loss incurred while the vehicle was in PIC hands. Now it was a case of making contact again with the stocky man in the stained overalls.

"That was the easy part," Alex said as he changed down a gear and turned the Freelander left into York Way. "If we're going to get anywhere with these people, we're going to have to be as cool as ice."

Maddie nodded as she slid slightly on the deep grey leather seat. "I can do cool," she said. She didn't tell Alex about the anxiety that was cramping her stomach. She kept her hands in her lap so he wouldn't see how they were shaking. It wasn't the operation that unnerved her; it was the thought of messing up – of making a bad move and wrecking everything. That was what dried her mouth and made the hairs on her neck prickle as Alex guided the Freelander along the narrow alley behind Apex Carwash.

He cut the engine and looked at her. "We can call this off if you're not ready," he said gently.

She stared at him, her eyes filling with streetwise insolence. "Let's do it," she said. She swung out of the vehicle and strolled over to the wooden gates in the viaduct.

They were closed. She hammered on them.

Alex came up alongside her.

A long, slow minute passed. The gate opened. The stocky man stared out at them.

Alex didn't speak. He just pointed towards the Freelander.

The man nodded. "Bring her inside," he said.

Alex walked back to the car. The man opened the double gates wide. Alex drove the Freelander inside.

Hanging fluorescent tubes lit the arched workshop. There were car parts strewn all over, benches and shelves of tools and spares, a smell of oil and petrol.

The man closed the gates and hammered bolts home.

Alex got out of the car and stood next to Maddie.

The man walked around the Freelander, leaning close here and there, as though checking things out, then he came back to where they were standing. "I didn't expect to see you two clowns again," he said. "She looks brand new. Where'd you get her?"

"You don't need to know," said Alex. "You wanted a Freelander – we got you one. It's even in the right colour."

"So where's our money?" Maddie demanded.

The man didn't even look at her. He was staring at Alex, as if trying to psyche him out.

Alex held his gaze.

The older man was the first to break eye contact. "Maybe we can work together, you and me," he said. "This was just a test run. You get money next time – if you make good. You can call me Ted. What's your name?"

"Alex. And she's Maddie."

Ted's eyes narrowed. "Get wise, Alex – ditch the girlfriend. Girls are no use around here."

Without warning, Maddie sprang forward and struck him with the heel of her hand in the centre of his sternum. Her foot hooked around behind his legs. He stumbled over backwards, unable to keep his balance. She came down heavily on top of him, grasping his extended arm, bringing her knee in hard to his shoulder, twisting his arm against the joint, folding his hand down and holding it there.

He struggled. The armlock tightened. He gasped with pain.

"Keep still and it won't hurt," Maddie said coldly. "You try to mess with me and I'll rip your arm off and beat you to death with it. You hear me?"

Ted nodded. His face was red. He was breathing hard. Sweat was forming on his forehead.

"We want our money," Maddie said. "Five hundred pounds. Now."

Alex leant over the man. "Maddie's a pretty useful girl to have around," he said, his voice smooth and calm. "What do you say?"

"OK," Ted gasped. "Get off me. I get the point. You'll have your money."

Maddie released his arm and jumped up. She glowered dangerously at him as he clambered heavily to his feet. He rubbed his shoulder, looking warily at her. But she could see a grudging respect in his eyes. She suddenly realised that her nerves had evaporated. This was going to work out just fine.

Ted reached into the back pocket of his overalls. He took out a wad of bank notes, peeled off five twenty-pound notes and handed them to Alex.

"One hundred?" Alex said.

"That's the starting rate," said the man. "You have to be on the team to get the full rate. You have to prove yourself."

"You want more proof that I can steal cars?" Alex said. "Listen to me, Ted. I worked for six months for a company that installed car security systems." He smiled. "I can disable any system on the market. Dual-zone shock sensors. Voltage-drop sensors. Ultrasonic remote protection. Engine immobilisers. Passive alarm systems. Anti-scan rolling code systems. I can get through the lot. Now stop messing us about – do we get on the payroll or do we go and offer our services to someone with brains?"

Ted eyed Alex with a half-smile. "You're a smart kid," he growled. "I like that. I'll tell you what I'll do for you. You go and spend that ton I've just given you, then meet up with me at six o'clock tonight. Not here. I'll give you the address."

He walked into the gloom at the back of the arch.

Maddie looked at Alex. "What are 'anti-scan rolling code systems'?" she whispered.

Alex winked. "I don't know," he said. "I saw them advertised on the Internet. Let's hope they don't want me to demonstrate how to override one. By the way – nice call with the jujitsu."

"I thought he needed a lesson in manners," Maddie murmured. "Do you think we're in?"

Alex nodded. "Oh, yes," he said. "We're in."

Chapter Six

PIC Control.

DCS Cooper's office.

Jack Cooper sat behind his desk. It was strewn with files and documents. His wheelchair was drawn up to the broad picture window. The London skyscape stretched out in front of him. He stared out over the city, deep in thought.

After several minutes he turned his chair to the desk again and pressed his intercom. "Tara? Come in here, please."

"Yes, sir."

Ten seconds later, Tara knocked and entered.

"Close the door behind you," Jack Cooper instructed. He pressed again to be put through to the Communications Centre. "No calls until further notice," he ordered.

He looked at Tara. She stood at his desk, tall and clear-eyed, waiting for her instructions. "What I am about to tell you," Jack Cooper began, "is for your ears only."

The expression on Tara's face didn't alter.

"Sit down," Jack Cooper told her. "We've got work to do."

⊗

Clerkenwell, EC1.

18:10.

It was a back street. High brick walls and shuttered doors. Cars were parked, but there was no through traffic. Alex and Maddie had been waiting there for nearly half an hour.

A grey Ford Sierra cruised into the street and drew to a halt. Ted got out.

There were no preliminaries. He beckoned to Alex and Maddie and they followed him to a side door in a blank wall. He produced a key and opened the door. The door closed automatically behind them.

He led them along a long, damp corridor to a concrete stairway. They went down three levels.

"What is this place?" Alex asked.

"It used to be a meat packer's," Ted replied. "Now it's called the Factory." He looked at Alex. "You'd better be prepared, kid. You're about to meet some very serious men."

A shiver ran down Maddie's spine.

Ted pushed open a set of heavy doors. They came into a great floodlit underground room, filled with noise and activity. Thick concrete pillars divided the Factory. It was full of men working on cars. Alex noticed the Freelander over to the left. It was being resprayed.

The vehicles were undergoing various transformations. Bonnets were open and men were filing down engine numbers. Security systems were being ripped out. Seats were being removed and new ones with different upholstery put in their place. Numberplates were being switched. Marked windows and headlamps were being taken out and substituted with untraceable ones.

Maddie could see why this place was referred to as the Factory. An entire criminal industry was in full swing down there. There had to be at least fifty cars in the Factory, with about a dozen men working on them.

A hollow-cheeked man with cold eyes and short dark hair approached them. "Who's this?" he asked sharply, glaring at Maddie and Alex.

"It's OK, Harry," said Ted. "They're a couple of new recruits. I thought Joe would want to give them the once-over. They're useful kids."

Harry's eyes flamed. "Are you out of your mind? Bringing strangers down here – especially at a time like this," he said. "You know the rules! No strangers at the Factory. Have you got a death wish or something?"

"These kids are OK," said Ted. "Believe me, Joe will want to see them."

Harry gave Alex and Maddie the evil eye. "The Boss never allowed anyone down here unless we knew they were clean," he snarled.

"The Boss?" said Ted. "Joe Davies is the boss, now, Harry, whether you like it or not. And if the old boss used to run things so well, how come he's a cold slab of meat in a mortuary right now?"

Maddie glanced at Alex. His eyes told her to stay quiet and keep listening. It was obvious that a change of leadership had recently occurred. And from what Ted was saying, it wasn't because of old age.

"That's a good question," Harry murmured under his breath. "Maybe someone got ambitious."

Ted's eyes narrowed. "I'd think twice before sounding your mouth off like that, Harry," he said. "Some people wouldn't find that joke very funny."

A third man appeared, tall and thin with a hard face and cunning eyes. "What joke's that?" he asked.

"No joke," said Harry. "Ted seems to think it's a great idea to bring sightseers down here." He moved away.

Joe Davies looked curiously at Maddie and Alex.

"What happened to the old boss?" Alex asked. "If people are getting killed, we don't want any part of it."

"Shut it!" Ted snarled. "Or I'll shut it for you."

Joe frowned at Alex. "You don't ask questions, boy. You answer them. I'm the boss. That's all you need to know. Ted? What's the story?"

"These are the kids that brought me the Freelander," Ted said. "Alex here says he knows all there is to know about security systems."

Joe looked at Alex. "How did you get the car?" he asked.

"I drove it out of the showroom in Park Lane," Alex said smoothly, repeating the story that he and Maddie had already agreed. "Maddie kept the salesman busy while I got the keys. I just took it out on to the road and put my foot down."

Davies's eyes turned to Maddie.

"I pretended I was ill," she said. "I collapsed in front of the salesman. While he was busy coping with that,

Alex took the car." She looked into his eyes. "It wasn't exactly brain surgery."

Joe Davies nodded. He looked at Alex again. "I can use you," he said.

"The girl knows some martial arts stuff," Ted said. "She's quick – stronger than she looks."

Joe eyed Maddie. "Muscle I've got in spades. It's skills I need." He smiled coldly at Maddie. "Sorry, little lady, but I need people who are handy with cars. I can't use people who don't know a spark plug from a hole in the ground." He turned away from her, dismissing her.

Maddie knew she had to pull back the situation, and quickly. She had an ace up her sleeve that even Alex didn't know about. "I know my way around cars," she said.

Joe Davies looked at her. "Really?" he said. His tone was completely flat. He began to walk away, but then turned and went towards a silver S-type Jaguar. He popped the bonnet and leant in over the engine. Maddie couldn't see what he was doing. When he straightened up he wiped his hands on a rag.

"Fix it," he challenged Maddie.

Maddie walked over to the car. She stared down at the engine for a few moments then opened the door and slid into the driver's seat. The keys were in the ignition. She turned the key. The engine turned over but didn't fire. There was no power.

Maddie smiled. She got out of the car again. She walked over to Davies, holding her hand out. "You took the rotary arm out of the distributor," she said. "Do you want me to put it back?"

Davies laughed. He dropped the small piece of metal into her hand. She went back to the car, took off the distributor cap and placed the arm in position. Then she brought the bonnet down with a clang.

She got into the car again and turned the engine on. It throbbed into life and purred like a tiger.

Maddie knew she had to prove herself beyond any shadow of doubt. She had to do something spectacular. She just hoped she was up to it.

She prepared herself, clearing her mind, letting memories of her driving course at Hendon flow into her mind. She knew Joe Davies and Ted were watching her. She looked at Alex. He gave a slight wink to show his support.

Maddie sucked in a deep breath and took the plunge. The Jaguar slid smoothly forwards. She kept her face expressionless – she couldn't let them see how nervous she was. She had to make this look effortless.

She sped up, steering the car around the perimeter

of the underground space, feeling everyone watching her.

Rapidly accelerating along the back wall of the warehouse, she headed straight for a parked car. The man working on it ran for his life. She grinned and braked hard, tyres screaming. She cracked the gear stick into reverse and – twisting to look over her shoulder – backed at speed along the wall. The Jaguar executed a perfect J-turn. She could hear Dane's voice in her head. "Keep your speed up!"

Maddie cornered fast as her confidence built. She had one more trick to perform. All she had to do was keep her head, time it right and trust her abilities.

She was on the home strait now – moving fast towards where Joe Davies and his two heavies were standing. Gripping the handbrake she counted down calmly. Three – two – one. Now!

She hauled on the handbrake and screeched to a halt, swinging the back of the car around in a howl of burning rubber. The car halted just a few centimetres from where Joe Davies stood. She cut the engine and sat for a moment – just until her heart rate settled a little and she felt sure her shaking legs would support her. Then she got out of the car, leaning over the roof, and gave Joe Davies a challenging stare.

He began to laugh.

There was scattered applause from the shop floor.

Maddie didn't smile. Hard expression. Hard eyes. Not a girl to be messed with.

Davies spread his hands. "OK," he said. "You can work for me. If you drive like that and don't damage the cars, you won't regret it." He looked out across the workshop. "Well, you've all got work to do," he said loudly.

The men got back to their tasks.

Maddie walked over to stand at Alex's side.

Davies looked at them. "Let's get you two started," he said.

Maddie glanced sideways at Alex. "That's what we're here for," she said.

⊗

A Bedford lorry carrying a humped shape covered in tarpaulin manoeuvred into the narrow back street. A line of dark cars followed it. The lorry aligned itself with a shuttered door in the wall. Men began to get out of the cars. Most of them were carrying baseball bats.

Four of the men climbed up the sides of the lorry and pulled off the tarpaulin to reveal a construction of steel scaffold poles that formed a wide battering ram.

The men heaved the construction so that it hung over the back of the van.

The men climbed off and the lorry drove forwards, then stopped. The driver put it into reverse and the lorry moved backwards, quickly picking up speed. It struck the steel shutter with a crash. The metal buckled. The lorry moved forwards and then reversed again.

This time, the shutter was swept aside with a scream of twisting metal.

The men pulled on dark masks. They began to pour in through the breech.

A long slope wound down to the Factory. The invaders ran down towards the lower levels.

Davies and his gang were about to get some unwanted visitors.

Chapter Seven

Deptford, SE8.

18:30.

It was a warm, humid evening. A white delivery van was parked in a side street off Creek Road. The warehouse – the target of the PIC stakeout – was two streets away.

There was no one in the front cab. Any passing pedestrian would think that the vehicle was unoccupied.

It wasn't.

Danny sat cocooned inside a nest of cutting-edge surveillance equipment. Banks of faders and monitor screens, rows of dials and touch-sensitive panels lined the inner walls of the van. Small red and green lights flashed constantly.

The Mobile Surveillance Unit was at work.

Danny checked the scanner, fine-tuning the frequency 'sniffer', on the lookout for hidden transmissions. The range was 100 kHz to 2000 MHz. It had a wide spectrum analyser and a booster pack designed by Danny himself, allowing it to scan 20 degrees above and below standard.

The 360-degree ESD9200 Laser Detector had picked up CCTV cameras operating at the front and the back of the warehouse. There was nothing unusual about that, but the presence of closed-circuit cameras meant that getting into the building to plant a bug would be tricky. Danny had decided to keep his investigations external, unless it became vital to get information from inside. He had managed to install a hidden camera with a motion-activated CMOS sensor. He had positioned it on the top of a two-metre high wall on the opposite side of the street from the main entrance. Considering that it was no bigger than Danny's thumb, the camera relayed pictures to Danny's laptop that were remarkably clear. Pinpoint accurate.

"OK," Danny murmured to himself as he double-checked his gear. "The lights have gone down, the audience is in its seats. Let's see some action."

There had been no activity from the warehouse since the MSU had arrived. The gates were locked. The windows barred and darkened. No one came. No one went.

Danny chewed his way thoughtfully through his third pack of M&Ms as the minutes ticked slowly by. He would be here till morning. It was going to be a long night.

The first anyone in the Factory knew of the attack was the crash of the shutter door being beaten down.

Davies ran forward. His hand slammed down on a wall-mounted control device. A steel-mesh grille began to descend across the entrance to the ramp.

All activity stopped. Mechanics looked up. Others were already running towards the exit at the far end.

Maddie and Alex moved towards each other, ready to make a united front against whatever was coming.

Davies tried shouting orders, but it was too late.

The first of the invading men reached the grille and jammed it open halfway. They were dressed in black, their faces hidden by ski masks. A whole flood of them seemed to follow, shouting and wielding baseball bats.

Ted ran forwards and was savagely beaten – he sank to his knees, his arms curled over his head in an attempt to protect himself. He was bleeding heavily from a cut on his jaw. Maddie's stomach flipped as she realised what they were up against.

She saw Davies duck into the Portakabin. Some of the Factory mechanics and workers had got over their surprise and were now moving forwards, armed with their heaviest tools – more like formidable opponents ready to make a fight of it.

It was chaos – like some kind of underground battlefield. Maddie and Alex were given no time for strategy. A baseball bat swung at head height. Alex ducked, driving one fist into the man's stomach, catching hold of the extended wrist and twisting it. The man doubled up, dropping the bat. Alex scooped the weapon up and turned to meet the next attacker.

Two thickset men came towards Maddie. All she could see were their menacing eyes staring wildly out at her from under their masks. She wasn't attacked. One of the men shouldered her aside. She was just a girl – not worth wasting their breath on.

Alex was warding off a violent assault, holding his own. Maddie saw another man move towards him. Two to one. Unfair odds. Maddie made her mind up in an instant.

She threw herself forwards, spinning to deliver a

mawashi geri – a roundhouse kick that sent the man staggering. A *mae geri* push-kick unbalanced him and an *empi uchi* elbow strike finished the job.

Alex's voice: "Maddie! Watch out!"

Maddie turned. Out of the corner of her eye she saw something rushing towards her. A baseball bat. She had become a target.

No time to think. Skill and instinct. Power and precision.

Sakotsu – osoto gari.

She could see the fear in the man's eyes as she caught him in an unbreakable armlock and then threw him. The club clattered to the floor. The winded man crawled away from her, gasping for breath. She picked up the fallen baseball bat and stood back-to-back with Alex.

Glass flew as windscreens were shattered. Lights were beaten in. Bonnets and wings dented and buckled.

Davies emerged from the Portakabin. Maddie saw an automatic pistol in his hand. He aimed it high. There was a burst of gunfire. The whine of ricochets. A fluorescent tube exploded.

There were shouts. The invaders began to run for the ramp.

Davies's voice rang out. "You tell Mr L that Joe

Davies wants a word!" he shouted after the retreating thugs. "You tell him I'm not such an easy target."

He pulled the trigger once more, aiming high again to scare rather than kill.

He took control, ordering his workers up the ramp, telling them to run a couple of cars across the entrance and to keep a watch, just in case anyone felt like coming back for more.

Ted had blood on his face, but no one else had been seriously hurt.

Alex eyed Davies as the tall man stood staring down at the devastation.

"Scum!" Davies snarled. He shouted up the ramp. "Next time it's for real! You hear me?"

Alex came up to his side. "Who were they?" he asked. "What the hell are we getting into?"

Davies smiled in grim triumph. "Competitors. They want to close us down. Don't worry about it. I'm ready for them." He patted Alex's shoulder. "Now isn't it time for you and your girlfriend to go steal us a few cars?"

⊗

The shadows were lengthening by the time Maddie and Alex left the underground warehouse. Evening was giving way to a city night, bright with neon and yellow streetlights.

"Scary stuff," said Maddie, looking back at the twisted wreckage of the shutter door. Two cars blocked the gaping entrance.

"It looks like we've landed right in the middle of a gang war," Alex said. "That could cause problems." He looked at her. "You handled yourself well in there."

"I take my vitamins," she said, smiling.

He nodded. "You're full of surprises, Maddie. Where did you learn to fix cars like that?"

"I used to help Dad when he did repairs and stuff on the family car," she said. "I picked things up."

"I noticed you also picked up how to do a handbrake turn," Alex said.

"Not bad, eh?" Maddie said.

Rapid footsteps approached from behind. It was Harry, running to catch up with them.

It suddenly occurred to Maddie that she hadn't seen him during the fight.

"Joe sent me after you," he said. "There's been a change of plan. We need a Mercedes CL600. It's a special job. We need it tonight."

Alex looked at him. A CL600 was a rare and highly expensive vehicle. "The streets are full of them, Harry," he said, his voice dripping with irony. "Sure you only want one? Any particular colour, or should I just go for one that matches your eyes?"

"You've got a mouth on you, kid," Harry snarled. He handed Alex a piece of paper. "The car we want is at this address. Joe wants it back here before midnight." His eyes glinted with malice. "And you two kids be careful. I'd hate for anything to happen to you."

He turned and walked back along the street.

Maddie shivered. He gave her the creeps.

"Nice guy," Alex said.

"If you like sewer rats," joked Maddie.

"That's just being unkind to sewer rats," Alex said as he studied the address. It was in St John's Wood. He glanced at Maddie. "So? Do we do it or do we pass?"

"We should make contact with Control," said Maddie. "We weren't told that we could go off and steal cars for real."

Alex nodded. "You're right. We should call them. But the way things are going, it looks like we're in for an interesting night."

Chapter Eight

PIC Control.

Duty Officer's work station.

Susan Baxendale was on night duty when the call came in from Alex and Maddie. She listened intently as Alex updated her. "Understood," she said. "I'll get someone on the gang-war angle and see what we can find out for you."

"What about the Merc?" Alex asked.

"Take it," Susan told him. "We don't have time to find a substitute or to make a switch. Besides, if you don't do it, Davies will send somebody else. I'll note it on file. If anything goes wrong, we'll reimburse the owner."

She put the phone down. Susan wasn't one for small talk, and she had plenty of work to do. Jack Cooper and his PA had gone to a meeting with the Secretary of State for Defence. Tara Moon had loaded her laptop with active files before she and the boss had driven off. Tara had said that they would be out of the office for a few days. No further details had been offered and Susan hadn't asked for any. If she needed to know, she would be told.

But one thing was clear: something was cooking. Something that not even Jack Cooper's most trusted deputies were being briefed on.

St John's Wood, NW8.

20:46.

The silver-grey Mercedes CL600 was parked on the forecourt of a large detached house. It gleamed in the fading light as Alex and Maddie stood on the far side of the street and considered their options.

Alex had pointed out a square external security light high on the front wall. "It's probably got a movement detector," he said. "We wouldn't get within ten metres of that car without setting the thing off."

"Is there no way of stopping the security light from operating?" Maddie asked.

Alex shook his head. "Not without the kind of gear that Danny carries around in the MSU," he replied.

"OK," said Maddie. "Here's the plan: I'll walk straight in there and ring the front door bell. That way, no one is going to be suspicious about the light firing up. You slip in behind me and do the business on the car. I'll apologise for disturbing whoever answers the door and say I'm looking for... uh..."

"Hamilton Terrace," Alex suggested. "That's just a couple of streets away."

"Fine. Got it. I ask them the way there. They tell me. I thank them. I walk off. They close the door and go back to watching EastEnders or whatever."

"And I break into the car and meet you on the corner with it," said Alex. He nodded. "Sounds good. Let's do it. I'll meet you on the corner with the Merc."

Five minutes earlier.

A stout, middle-aged man sat in his Finn Juhl leather Chieftain armchair. Anthony Longman was alone in the room. His family were at home in Essex. Longman had leased the house in St John's Wood from an agency – it was a comfortable place to stay on the occasions when work kept him in town overnight.

The living room had been designed with the

greatest care and style. A Persian rug lay on the polished floorboards. A Poul Kjærholm steel and glass table. A Verner Panton lamp. Each item of furniture placed to maximum effect.

Longman was watching the latest James Bond movie on a huge wall-mounted screen. In his hand he was slowly warming a glass of Domaine de Baraillon Bas Armagnac, the heady aroma rising as he savoured each sip.

The telephone rang.

He frowned, pausing the DVD – the Secret Service agent was caught in midair, his guns blazing silently.

Longman picked up.

⊗

Harold Green was also alone, but in far less pleasant surroundings. He stood in a cold, shabby office, staring down into a darkened street. He smiled unpleasantly. He held his mobile phone to his ear, waiting for his call to be answered.

Harry was going to be busy over the next few hours. Some old debts needed repaying – and if everything went according to plan, by the morning things would be back the way they had been in the good old days.

There was a click as the line opened.

⊗

Anthony Longman put down the phone. He picked up another remote control, pressed a button and the living-room lights dimmed to a glimmer. He stood up and walked to the window – keeping to one side, moving cautiously.

Staring down into the broad forecourt of the house he frowned. His six-week-old Mercedes was still where he had left it. He walked to the door and called out.

Two men appeared from another room.

Longman's voice was low and mellow. "I've just been given a tip off that Joe Davies is going to nick my Merc tonight," he purred. "Go and check things out, boys. If you find anyone nosing about out there – a young kid and his girlfriend, apparently – bring them up here. I want a word with them."

The two men headed down the stairs. "Oh, and watch out for the girl," Longman called after them. "Apparently she's got claws."

One of the men drew out a Bowie knife and smiled. Razor sharp. He grinned. His gold-capped canine glinted in the light reflected from the steel edge.

"No filleting tonight, Raymond," Longman said. "I want to talk to them, not eat them!"

Longman went back to his movie, closing the door behind him. He moved over to a small grey box fixed on to the wall, opened it and operated the internal override for the security lights.

That would lull the two young thieves into a false sense of security. So much more amusing, then, when his two men came down on them like a ton of bricks.

And to think he had been planning a quiet night in front of the television.

Chapter Nine

Maddie was halfway across the broad forecourt, gravel crunching underfoot. The security light had still not come on. Maybe it was malfunctioning. Maybe the people who lived in the house hadn't set the system yet.

Glancing over her shoulder she could just make out Alex's shadow by the brick gatepost.

As she reached the front doorstep the light still hadn't activated so there was no need to ring the bell. She looked around. She saw Alex gliding low towards the silver-grey car. He disappeared behind it.

The headlights blinked three times. He had deactivated the alarm.

Maddie tensed. Nervous. This was too easy.

She could hear faint sounds as Alex used his PIC-learnt trick to open the car door. He slid into the driver's seat.

Maddie heard a soft, sharp sound behind her. She turned. Cold shock flared through her. The front door was half-open. A muscular man loomed. A broad knife-blade flashed. Hands caught her and held her before she could act. She felt a sharp metal edge at her throat.

A second man stepped past her.

Alex realised that something had gone wrong when he climbed out of the car. He stared towards the house and saw the knife at Maddie's throat.

Closing the car door, he dropped the alarm disabler and back-heeled it into the bushes that lined the front wall of the forecourt.

Keeping his face impassive, he raised his hands in surrender.

The man came around the front of the car.

"I suppose a test drive is out of the question," Alex said.

⊗

Deptford.

21:28.

The MSU.

Danny sipped his espresso. It was the best way for him to stay alert through the long, solitary vigil. A quick fix of caffeine kept him awake for hours.

As darkness fell the streetlights came on one by one. The occasional car or van rumbled past.

Danny hummed to himself as he sketched a circuit diagram for a new interference damper on a note pad to pass the long, quiet minutes.

A flicker of movement caught his attention. The CMOS sensor kicked in, lighting up the screen of Danny's laptop with a picture of the front of the warehouse.

"Hello, there," Danny murmured to himself, his mind instantly focused. "I think we have some visitors."

A dark car had parked in the shadows between two streetlights. Danny couldn't make it out. Two men walked quickly towards the side door of the warehouse. They stood for a few moments in the doorway. Danny frowned. They had their backs to him. He'd have to wait until they came out again to get a good view of their faces. The door opened and closed behind them.

Danny had no way of listening in on conversations – his long-range microphone needed a clear line of sight, not possible from such a distance. But if the men used any kind of intercom or mobile phone, he'd be able to pick them up on the frequency scanner.

"You should have put a bug in there," he chided himself. "Big mistake."

He waited, tense and ready. He watched the lights and display panels. He reached blindly for his fourth pack of M&Ms. He chewed slowly.

A frequency display peaked suddenly. He recognised the configuration. Someone was using a mobile.

"Yes!" Danny hissed. He tuned the instrument.

A voice sounded in his earphones. "...the General that everything is ready. We've examined the merchandise and it's exactly as specified. Everything is secure and ready for transport."

A second voice: "I'll pass the message on. Arrangements are being made. I'll contact you with the details as soon as everything has been finalised."

The frequency display levelled out. The call was over.

Danny leant back in his seat. "Now, I wonder who the General might be," he mused.

Maddie and Alex were taken up the stairs. The knife was no longer at Maddie's throat, but it was still in Raymond's hand – a constant threat.

Alex came quietly, watching and waiting. Something

didn't ring true about all of this. A person discovering that their car is about to be stolen doesn't usually abduct the would-be thieves at knifepoint.

Maddie's thoughts were racing along similar lines. This whole thing reeked of a set-up. But why had they been set up? What had they stumbled into?

They came to the landing. A portly man stood in a doorway.

"No problems, Mr L," said Raymond. "They were as good as gold."

Mr L. Maddie heard Davies's voice, shouting in her head. *You tell Mr L that Joe Davies wants a word!* She had a moment of clarity. Two rival car rings. One run by Mr L. The other one run by Joe Davies. The orders to steal the Merc hadn't come from Davies. Harry had set it up. He was using them to light a fire under Mr L – working to bring Davies down.

Maddie looked at the man. He had a round, cherubic face, but his eyes were small and hard. He seemed the kind of man who would take the theft of his own car very seriously. He was probably behind the death of Davies's predecessor. Maddie had the bad feeling that things were spinning out of control.

Mr L moved back into the room. Maddie and Alex were pushed forwards.

He stared at them, weighing them up, deciding what to do with them.

"I was watching you," he told Alex, gesturing towards the window that overlooked the forecourt. "How did you get into my car so quickly? I timed it. Eight seconds. No one can break into a Mercedes CL600 in eight seconds."

Alex looked at the man. "I can," he said.

Mr L nodded. "So it would seem." He approached Alex, peering closely at him with a chilling smile. "I was planning on having Raymond and Toby here beat the two of you to a pulp and then throw you off Vauxhall Bridge."

Maddie had got over the shock and the fear of the knife. It was time to take the initiative. "But you'd be making a mistake," she said. "Alex is the best – and we work as a team."

Mr L shifted his gaze from Alex to Maddie, then back again.

Alex stared back. He had come to the same conclusion as Maddie. The only way for them not to become casualties of this gang war was to convince Mr L that they were worth employing.

"There isn't a car in the world we can't get into," Alex said. "Mr Davies is a loser. Maddie and I want to sit at the big boys' table."

"Or you could have us thrown off the bridge," Maddie added. She shrugged. "Your loss."

Mr L began to laugh. He sat down, still laughing.

Maddie was uneasy. This could go either way. Either he would finish laughing and then set his thugs on them or...

"I like you," Mr L said at last. He was smiling widely. "I can always use new talent." He looked beyond them. "Raymond? Take these kids to Shoreditch. Tell Mortimer to put them to work."

He turned back to the giant television screen. The image was still frozen. He pressed the remote, and digital stereo gunfire filled the room as James Bond finished his long leap.

The job interview was over.

Chapter Ten

Shoreditch, E8.

Midnight.

Maddie was wide awake, alert to her fingertips, psyched up for whatever was to come next. She could almost taste the danger as Toby drove them across London. She sat in the front passenger seat, Alex in the back with Raymond. The journey was undertaken in complete silence.

They parked in Brick Lane and Toby waited in the car while Raymond led them up to a shabby little first-floor office. He left them there without a word.

A man sat behind a desk. A computer screen glowed in stand-by mode.

The man was in his mid-forties, impeccably dressed in a Turnbull & Asser suit and silk tie. Maddie didn't think he would have looked out of place at one of the trading desks in the City Futures Market.

Alex looked at him. "Are you Mortimer?" he said.

The man's expression didn't flicker. "It's *Mr* Mortimer, usually," he said disdainfully, in a voice that was as well groomed as his suit. "And your names would be?"

"I'm Alex – she's Maddie."

Mr Mortimer looked carefully at her. "I see," he said. "No last names?"

"The guy in St John's Wood said you'd give us work," Alex said. "You want us to fill in a couple of employment forms first? I'm Alex Smith. She's Maddie Brown. You can put us both down as no fixed address."

"You've been working for Mr Davies, I believe?" said Mr Mortimer.

"We did one job," said Alex. "That was it. Mr L looked like he could afford to pay us better." Alex grinned. "What's with the 'Mr L' business – has he got a stupid name or something?"

Mr Mortimer didn't respond. He looked keenly into their faces.

Alex got the impression that he was a very sharp man. They would have to be careful.

The phone rang. "Excuse me," Mr Mortimer said. He picked up. He didn't speak. He listened for no more than ten seconds then put the phone down again.

"Wrong number?" Maddie asked.

"Far from it," Mr Mortimer replied. He relaxed back in his chair. "In fact, I'd say you jumped ship just in time, Miss Brown. Things are getting quite exciting over at the Factory."

Alex and Maddie glanced at one another.

What was going on?

⊗

The Factory.

Clerkenwell.

Davies was busy in the Portakabin. After the boss had been murdered, he had been quick to slap Harry Green down and take over the business. But all the admin didn't have the buzz of being out there on the streets.

A dozen or more men were working on the cars late into the night. There was a lot of damage to put right. A baseball bat can do a lot of harm to a £150,000 car.

Davies also needed to make some contingency plans for when his enemies came back. Mr L had been desperate to shut them down ever since the boss had set this business up. The two gangs were bitter enemies – mainly because the boss had been Mr L's right-hand man until he decided to go it alone.

And then the boss had got a bullet in his head. Davies smiled grimly. Careless – making yourself an easy target like that.

Davies wasn't going to be got rid of that easily. He had to make a few phone calls. Reel in some old favours. Get some heavy muscle. Fight back. And he had to make sure Harry Green was on board. The guy had wanted to take over the business himself. There had been bad blood. It was time to put things right.

Davies leant out of the Portakabin.

"Anyone seen Harry?" he asked.

No one had.

Joe Davies sat back down. His face contracted in a frown. He hadn't seen Harry all night – not since the attack. Where was he?

There was a muffled roar from the other side of the huge warehouse. It startled Davies out of his thoughts. He stared through the window. A bloom of dark smoke came from one of the cars. A flare of red flame. Davies's eyes widened.

A second explosion shook the floor. Much closer. A BMW 5 had burst into flames. No one was near it. Harry had been working on that car earlier in the day.

Smoke billowed out. Everyone was shouting. Running. Coughing.

Davies stood in the doorway of the Portakabin. "Harry!" he whispered, his voice full of cold fury. "You're a dead man!"

⊗

Harry Green gazed down from the window of the darkened office. He looked at his watch.

Any moment now.

He stared into the street. Two cars had been parked nose-to-nose to block the place where the shutter door had been smashed in. He could see men sitting in the cars. Wary and nervous – but totally unprepared for what was about to hit them.

A fleet of dark blue Vectras swept around the corner. Quiet as prowling sharks. No sirens at first – not until all exits had been blocked.

Then the two-tones began to wail and the blue lights flashed. The Flying Squad had arrived right on cue.

Harry hummed to himself as he watched the scene unfold beneath him. He smiled.

People came running up out of the Factory, calling to one another, coughing and stumbling into the road. Smoke, thought Harry. Good. The firebomb had done its job – sweet as candy.

He was waiting for one particular face to appear.

There he was – staggering around – trying to get clear. Running scared. Harry grinned as a policeman brought Davies down and cuffed him right there in the gutter.

Perfect. Harry reached for his mobile. He had some good news to pass on.

⊗

"Tell me about yourselves," said Mr Mortimer. "I like to know the people I employ."

Maddie stared insolently at him. "I thought that Mr L guy was employing us," she said.

Mr Mortimer smiled. "He rarely gets involved with the day-to-day running of the business. He leaves all that to me." His eyes narrowed. "I want to know where you two come from. And if I don't get some straight answers I'm going to toss you back to Raymond and Toby. Have I made myself quite clear?"

"Absolutely," Alex said, holding his hands up in a gesture of peace. "We're from Southend – both of us. We've been living rough for months – squatting, shoplifting, making a bit of money here and there." He went on to tell the story of the pub in Stepney. Their attempts to get on Davies's payroll. The way they were set up by Harry.

Mr Mortimer smiled at the mention of his name. "Ah, Harry," he said. "Salt of the earth. Loyal to a fault."

"I think maybe you're talking about a different Harry," said Maddie. "The one we met was pure sleaze."

Mr Mortimer inclined his head a little. "Harry Green was an employee of mine some time ago, but he decided to go and work for a rival firm. Fortunately he's now seen the error of his ways. He's doing a little job for me..." he paused, checking his watch, "right about now." He looked from Alex to Maddie. "You say you have nowhere to live?"

"We have a room in Tower Hamlets," Alex replied.

"I think perhaps I can do a little better than that," Mr Mortimer said. "There are some flats in Elephant and Castle." He opened a drawer. Inside there were a number of small envelopes. He took one out and handed it to Maddie. She could feel a hard shape inside. A key. An address was scribbled on the front of the envelope.

"They're basic," Mr Mortimer continued. "But you'll have running water and a roof over your heads. And if everything works out between us, you should soon be in a position to set yourselves up in a nice little place of your own."

The phone rang again. This time Mr Mortimer did speak.

"Yes, Harry. Good. Mr L will be very pleased to hear that. Of course, Harry – all is forgiven. Welcome back to the fold. I'll see you tomorrow." He put the phone down.

"What's happened?" Alex asked.

"Davies's little Factory has just closed," Mr Mortimer replied. "Permanently." He looked at them. "It's late. Take yourselves off to the Elephant. I want the two of you to report to me at eight o'clock tomorrow morning at the Peacock Dealership in Haverstock Hill, Belsize Park."

"Where's that?" Maddie asked. They were only supposed to have been in London for a few weeks – she wanted to give the impression that they didn't know their way around yet.

Mr Mortimer looked at her. "You find out. Think of it as an initiative test." He stood up. "I would appreciate it if you could arrive promptly in the morning."

Alex nodded. "We'll be there," he confirmed. "Eight sharp."

⊗

Danny's fingers rattled impatiently on the worktop. "I've got a whole van full of cutting-edge surveillance gear," he muttered to himself. "And what do I get out of it? Diddly-squat!"

The two men had left the warehouse within minutes of their phone call. Their car had snaked off into the night. He had got a few good shots of their faces. A file search on his laptop had come up empty. The two men weren't on the PIC database. And since then – nothing.

Midnight had come and gone. Danny drank his eighth coffee. He doodled on his note pad. He checked and double-checked that every monitor was working at peak efficiency. But his mind was elsewhere. "We have to put a bug inside that place," he said to himself at last.

He reached for the button that would patch him through to Control. He would need permission to go into the warehouse. "On the other hand," he said, drawing his hand back. "What Cooper doesn't know about, he won't worry about." He sat there for a few moments, turning the idea over in his head.

He gave a decisive nod and opened a carry-box. He picked out a MT50 bug. It looked like a double-socket telephone adaptor. It had a transmitter range of 200 metres and could be picked up on the MSU receiver – a KCR-1800, which had the facility to record twenty-four hours of information without needing a change of disk. Danny slipped the bug into his pocket.

He chose a few more precision tools and opened the

rear door of the van. The night air was cool as he stepped down into the road. Having silently closed the van he set the ultra-high-security alarm. He dug his hands deep into his pockets and set off.

It was time for some action.

Chapter Eleven

Step one: Danny cut carefully into the CCTV cable and attached a device that created a five-minute freeze-frame effect. He would easily be able to retrieve this later and patch the cable to leave no trace.

Step two: he crossed the road and checked out the entrance. Dead lock. Banham lock. Digital alarm box. He recognised it. Standard issue. No problem. Once the door was open, he would have fifteen seconds to tap in the correct four-digit number.

Step three: Danny slid the electronic key into the dead lock. A wire led from the key to a hand-held control box. He activated it and heard the click of the key engaging inside the lock. He turned the key to disengage the bolt. The Banham went the same way. He opened the door and closed it behind himself.

Danny counted down from fifteen in his head as he moved to the alarm box. Fourteen seconds. He flipped the cover. Eleven seconds. He took out a small black box. Nine seconds. He attached miniature bulldog clips to specific terminals. Five seconds. An LED screen flickered. Three seconds. The numbers appeared one by one. One second.

Danny tapped in the code. The alarm disengaged.

He was in.

⊗

Danny was standing in a two-storey building with storage space on the ground floor and offices up above. He slipped a powerful Maglite out of his pocket. Its narrow beam was surprisingly bright. His heart was beating fast as he made his way through a series of small rooms and down a flight of stairs. He opened a door and was confronted by a large stretch of darkness.

His torch picked out a crate. "Bingo!" Danny said with a grin.

There were twenty crates. Danny guessed that they were each about two metres long. A metre deep. A metre wide. Stencilled in black: AGRICULTURAL EQUIPMENT.

Just like Fly had told him.

Danny hunted around for a hammer. It was risky. The longer he stayed in there, the more likely he was to get caught. But he wanted to know exactly what was in those boxes. Heavy artillery, Fly had said.

Danny found a claw hammer and prized open a lid. The crate was packed with polystyrene balls. Danny shovelled them aside. A dark green barrel appeared, as thick as a drainpipe. Danny frowned as he uncovered more of the equipment. Even in its dismantled form, he could tell that it was some kind of missile launcher.

He went to another of the crates, jemmied the lid and scrabbled through the packaging. He let out a low whistle.

It was a missile.

Danny had seen enough. He closed the crates and hammered them down. Making his way cautiously to the front of the building, he found a telephone socket. The phone was live. Good. He fitted the bug.

Five minutes later he was back in the MSU, working on his laptop, looking for information. "That's the one," he murmured, as a picture of a missile and a launcher appeared. Specifications scrolled down on screen.

STARSTREAK HVM (High Velocity Missile)

Shoulder launch capability. Developed to engage

with high-performance, low-flying aircraft and attack helicopters. The missile employs three dart projectiles, allowing multiple hits.

Length of missile: 1.39 m.

Diameter: 0.27 m.

Speed: Mach 3+

Range: 4 km

"Just what every wannabe terrorist would like to have fall out of his cereal box," Danny said to himself. He shook his head. "Sorry to disappoint you guys – but these toys aren't going anywhere."

⊗

The Elephant and Castle, SE17.

South London.

The empty flat was much worse than Mortimer had described it. It was on the second floor of a long, narrow block. Crumbling concrete. Graffiti. Rubbish. Bad smells.

But it made sense for Maddie and Alex to go there, just in case there were any suspicious eyes on them. They had talked their way in, but that didn't mean that they were trusted.

It was a long journey south of the river. They still had Ted's one hundred pounds. The night bus had dropped them off fifty metres from their new home. It was three thirty in the morning.

"It stinks," said Maddie.

"No one's lived here for years," said Alex as they looked round the flat.

"Well it certainly smells as if something *died* here recently," Maddie replied.

"Probably condemned," said Alex, nudging a lump of rolled-up carpet with his foot. He crouched and drew the slimline mobile phone out of the side of his sock. It was time to make contact with Control.

They had plenty of information to report.

⊗

Maddie lay fully clothed on a narrow damp mattress in the filthy bedroom of the flat. She had a blanket half over her. Her hands were clasped behind her head. She was supposed to be asleep. It was four thirty – and they had to be in Belsize Park by eight.

She couldn't sleep. She guessed that Alex was probably having the same problem in the living room. He didn't even have a mattress to lie on – just the roll of carpet.

Too much had happened. Maddie's brain was whirling. Sifting information. Organising data. Trying to make sense of everything.

The call to Control had produced some feedback on the house in St John's Wood. It was owned by an absentee Saudi billionaire. Susan Baxendale had said she thought that the property was probably left in the hands of a letting agency, but there was no way of getting any information on that until the morning. Their description of Mr L led nowhere. Susan had said she would send a couple of agents over to the house to covertly check the place out.

How about the dead gang boss?

Nothing so far – still searching on that one.

Maddie heard faint sounds of movement from the living room. "Alex?" she called. "Are you awake?"

"No."

She smiled. "Neither am I," she called again. "It's been a weird kind of day, hasn't it?"

"It certainly has," Alex called back. "Listen – get some sleep if you can, Maddie. It's our first day in a brand new job tomorrow – we want to make a good impression."

Maddie looked at her watch. The hands glowed in the darkness. "Tomorrow?" she said. "Alex – we've got to be there in four hours."

"Get some sleep."

"You too."

She turned on to her side and pulled the foul-smelling blanket up as near to her face as she could stand.

Even a couple of hours of sleep would be better than nothing.

⊗

Deptford.

Sunday.

06:00.

Danny rubbed his tired eyes. The CMOS sensor was active again. The early morning light was pale and the shadows were still long. A car had pulled up outside the warehouse building. The same two men.

"The early bird catches the worm," Danny murmured. "Even a bleary-eyed bird that's been up all night drinking espresso." He yawned. He could use a shower and a change of clothes. Not just yet, though.

The two men entered the warehouse.

Danny's fingers played over dials. He smiled. The sound of two sets of footsteps was coming through his headset loud and clear.

⊗

PIC Control.

Susan Baxendale was snatching a few minutes sleep in the duty officer's rest room. Lying on the narrow bunk, dozing like a cat – one ear alert for the sound of the phone.

It rang at precisely 06:19. Susan picked up in two

rings. It was Danny. A call from the MSU. "I've got something," he told her. "There are two guys in the warehouse. They received a call at zero-six-ten. Apparently the General wants to check the goods before they're shipped out. He's coming over here at midday."

"Understood." Susan Baxendale was wide awake now. "I'll organise a snatch squad. Under your command. You're due a break – I'll send Gina over to relieve you."

"Fly was right about what's in there. There's a whole bunch of Starstreak missiles, along with their launchers. I've seen 'em. It's heavy stuff."

Susan's eyes narrowed. "You went in?"

"Uh... yes."

"Against orders?"

"Kind of."

Susan's mind came straight back on track. "How many agents do you think you'll need?"

"Safe side... a dozen," said Danny.

"I'll organise it. Danny?"

"Yo?"

"As soon as this operation is over, I want you in my office to discuss your attitude to command protocols."

"Looking forward to it already."

Susan put the phone down. She had work to do.

⊗

Belsize Park, NW3.

Haverstock Hill.

Peacock's Car Dealership.

The broad showroom windows stretched for twenty-five metres along the northeast facing side of the road. White stone. Red, white and blue pennants fluttered in the breeze. Glass and chrome gleamed. Behind the spotless windows stood a row of top-of-the-range luxury cars. Rollers. Bentleys. BMWs. Polished bodywork reflected the sunlight.

Alex and Maddie entered the plush showrooms. A night sleeping in their clothes had added some authenticity to their disguises – as had their early morning cold-water wash. Maddie's scalp was beginning to itch. Her hair felt rank. Working undercover was bad for personal hygiene.

They mentioned Mortimer's name and a smartly dressed salesman led them to a pair of swing doors.

"Down there," he said, not bothering to disguise his distaste. "And from now on, you come in through the back entrance."

They descended the stone stairs into a bare, damp-stained stairwell. Rusting iron rails. A far cry from all the opulence that was on show out front.

They came to closed double doors. There was a bell and a coded entry panel.

"This is the real thing," Alex murmured. "It makes the Factory look like a backyard operation."

Maddie nodded. Up above – all the respectability of an exclusive North London dealership. Down here – something else entirely. She rang the bell.

A short man in overalls opened the door. Beyond him they saw an expanse twice the size of the Factory in Clerkenwell. Brightly lit. Full of cars and mechanics. The smell of oil and petrol and fresh paint mingled with the smell of expensive leather and wax polish.

The small man led them to an office. Mortimer was in there speaking on the phone. Alex and Maddie were waved inside. Mortimer gestured for them to sit. The small man closed the door and left them to it.

Mortimer finished his call. He checked the wall clock and smiled. "Fifteen minutes early," he said. "Enthusiastic. I like that."

"We gave ourselves plenty of time," said Alex. "We thought maybe the Carnival would slow things down."

It was the weekend of the annual Notting Hill Carnival. Up to two million visitors were expected. Parts of West London would grind to a standstill for the two-day festival.

Mortimer shook his head. "That won't affect us here." He rubbed his hands together, elbows on the desk. "Now then, what shall we have you do?"

"We steal cars," Maddie said. "What did you have in mind? Fetching lunch?"

Mortimer frowned slightly. "You made a good impression on the chief. I'm not sure why." He looked at Alex. "He'll be paying us a visit, by the way. He would like a demonstration of exactly how you deal with high-tech vehicle security systems."

Maddie felt a coldness in her stomach. They had been dreading this. Alex did have some knowledge of how to get into locked cars – and of how to override the ignition. But without the alarm disabler, he wouldn't be able to get past wired-in microchip security.

Alex's reply gave no hint of his anxiety. "I'm ready when he is. When will he be here?"

"Later this afternoon," Mortimer said. "Meanwhile, go and see Peter – the gentleman who let you in. He's my foreman. He'll find you some work. Oh, and by the way, there are three important rules down here. Do what you're told. Don't leave the premises without permission. And don't ask questions. You'd be wise to remember them."

They left Mortimer's office. Peter had his head under

the open bonnet of an ice-blue Rolls Royce Corniche. Alex leant in close to Maddie as they walked towards him. "As soon as Mr L arrives, we're blown," he whispered. "If we get separated, find out anything you can about who he is and where he lives when he's not in St John's Wood."

Maddie nodded. She knew they had to work fast – time would soon be running out for Alex Smith and Maddie Brown of Southend.

Chapter Twelve

Alex's head was under the open bonnet of a red Maserati 3200 GT Assetto Corsa. He was filing down the engine number. It was just one of the methods used to disguise a stolen vehicle before passing it on to a new owner. A grey-haired, stick insect of a man leant against the front wing, watching Alex as he worked.

Kenny the Cleaner. Alex guessed that the small, wiry guy had to be in his late sixties. He had skin like an old lizard and big, sad, wet eyes. His overalls were two sizes too big for him. He leant on a broom. He never stopped talking.

Within a few minutes, Alex learnt that Kenny had

been in and out of prison all his life. A failed petty crook, he had known the Richardson gang back in the 1950s when he had been a hungry kid running errands for the criminal overlords of South London.

"Do you know much about motors, Alex?" Kenny asked.

"I get by," Alex said.

Kenny stroked the gleaming red metalwork of the wing. "She's a beauty, isn't she? I bet she eats petrol though. What do you think?"

Alex was suspicious that Kenny had been sent over to pump him for information. He decided to play along.

"She'll make 0 to 100 in 5.12 seconds," he said. "Top speed of 300 kph. She's fitted with Bilstein shock absorbers and Pagid RS421 high-attrition brake pads. She has Pirelli P-Zero Corsa tyres that hold the road like nothing else on Earth." He stood up and brought the bonnet down. "And this colour is called Rosso Mondiale." He smiled. "Have I passed?"

Kenny chuckled. "You know motors, all right, Alex," he said.

"You'd better believe it!" said Alex.

The telephone rang in Mortimer's office. He picked up, listened, then smiled. "Yes, sir. Thank you for letting me know. Yes. I think you made a wise move there. We were never going to be able to trust Harry again." He paused. "Yes. They're here. Peter's keeping them busy. Are you speaking from home, sir – in case I need to contact you later? Yes? Good. When will you be leaving? Yes, that's fine. They'll be here when you arrive. No I don't think so, but if we do have any problems, Raymond will deal with them. Goodbye, sir."

He put the phone down.

A body turned slowly, face down in the river under Vauxhall Bridge. A police launch was drawing close. An officer of the river police held a billhook out over the side, ready to catch the drowned man and haul him aboard.

Except that the floating man hadn't died from inhaling river water. Harry Green's throat had been cut.

The underground workshop was kitted out like a mini car factory. There was an inspection pit. Hydraulic jacks. A tyre-changing machine. Electric winches for moving engine blocks. Hand-built equipment that would disguise the stolen cars in as short a time as possible. Turnover was fast, efficient and very lucrative.

Alex was told to change all four tyres on a Ferrari F355 Spider.

Kenny was still haunting him. It was obvious now that the old man had been told to keep an eye on him. Alex was friendly enough – maybe Kenny would open up and provide some useful information.

Alex attached the electric spanner to the last wheel and pressed the trigger. The nuts spun. He put the device back on its rest. He straightened up. Time to ask Kenny a few questions.

Then Alex saw the car standing by itself in a bay. He didn't show by the slightest flicker that the yellow Bentley Continental T had special significance to him, but his eyes were on the car as he moved around the Ferrari. It didn't seem that any work had been done on it so far. The number plates were still the same as in the file that Jack Cooper had given them three days ago.

It was Robert Fraser's stolen car.

Alex wiped his hands. He needed to play this very cool. "That's a nice motor," he said, nodding towards the vehicle. "I've always had a soft spot for Bentleys." He smiled at Kenny. "I'm going to get myself a Continental T one of these days."

He walked slowly over to the car.

Kenny trailed after him, dragging his broom. "That one belonged to a guy who used to work here," Kenny said. "Mr Fraser. Smart man. Too smart for his own good. He was a classy guy, though. Public schoolboy gone bad."

"What happened to him?" Alex asked, playing it dumb.

"He went solo. Mr Mortimer was spitting blood, calling him all the names under the sun. Mr Fraser set up a rival firm, get it? Stupid thing to do if you want a long life."

"So what happened to him?" Alex probed.

Kenny frowned. "The way I heard it, Mr Mortimer sent a few boys out to give him a hiding and to bring his motor in. A warning, yeah? Get out of the business or get out of town. But something went wrong. Mr Fraser got shot. Dead."

"Over-enthusiastic boys," Alex said dryly.

Kenny shook his head. "No. It wasn't the boys that shot him. They weren't even tooled-up. Mr Fraser was shot by someone else."

"Like who?" Alex asked.

They had reached the car.

Kenny gave him an odd look. "You're a bit keen on knowing all this stuff aren't you? What was he to you, eh?"

Alex spread his hands. He needed to be careful. "Nothing – just interested that's all," he said casually. He tried to make a joke of it. "Bit of shop-floor gossip, eh?"

This idea seemed to appeal to Kenny, who leant closer. "Well, as it turns out, it wasn't Mr Mortimer," he said. "And it wasn't Mr L, neither. The big boss, when he wants someone topped, uses Raymond Pallow – and Raymond is a knife-man. Always. A Bowie knife. It's his trademark."

"I've met Raymond," Alex said.

"He's a nutter," Kenny croaked. "A psycho."

Alex peered in through the windows of the Bentley. "What happens to any stuff that's in the cars when they're lifted?" he asked. "The owner's personal stuff."

"That depends on what it is," Kenny replied. "Peter got me to clean this job out when it arrived. There was the usual junk. I dumped it." He pointed to a workbench at the back of the bay. "That briefcase was in there. One of the boys had grabbed it. I s'pose he thought there might have been a laptop or a mobile phone in it."

"And was there?" Alex asked.

"Nah. Nothing like that. Just a load of papers. Mr Fraser was some kind of civil servant."

Papers. No mention of a diary. Alex needed to see inside that briefcase.

"Oh, yeah," Kenny added. "And there was one of those computer games. Funny name, it had. Nemesis

3000. I handed that over to a friend of ours. Norma. She sells knocked-off stuff like that. She's a good girl. She runs an electrics shop on Chalk Farm Road."

Someone called for Kenny. Oil had been spilled. Kenny was sent off to get a mop and bucket.

Alex was alone for a few moments. He glided over to the back of the bay. He opened the briefcase and checked inside. Brown Manila folders. The documents inside were printed on official Ministry of Defence headed paper. Specialist Procurement Service. Departmental information and instructions.

Nothing useful.

He ran trained fingers around the inner surfaces of the case – seeking out any hidden compartments or pockets. There were none. He moved away, not wanting to be caught nosing around back there.

He was thinking fast. Jack Cooper's MoD contact was convinced that there would be some information in that briefcase, but Alex hadn't found anything. According to Kenny the Cleaner, the only thing taken out of that case had been a computer game disk – Nemesis 3000. If someone wanted to disguise vital data, what better way than to hide it on a fake games disk? Alex needed to get his hands on that disk. It could contain information that would expose Hydra UK.

Operation Hubcap had just taken an unexpected turn.

⊗

Maddie had been given the job of tidying up racks of shelving. Putting boxes of spares in some kind of order. Menial stuff. But it suited her – the shelves were close to Mortimer's office. She could hear most of what went on in there.

She heard the phone call with the person Mortimer called 'sir' – Maddie assumed he was talking to Mr L. One particular comment from Mortimer concerned her. *I think you made a wise move there. We were never going to be able to trust Harry again.*

Somehow, that sounded ominous. What had happened to Harry? And what had Mortimer meant when he had said: *...if we do have any problems, Raymond will deal with them.*

Maddie had a nasty feeling that Mortimer had meant problems with Alex and her. The memory of Raymond's knife at her throat chilled her blood.

She saw Alex, away over on the far side of the shop floor, talking to an old fellow with a broom. She wanted to make contact. They had known all along that this operation was potentially dangerous, but if her suspicions were correct, they were in far greater peril than they had anticipated. Maddie had the scary feeling that Harry was dead. One slip and they would go the same way.

She decided to play it cool for the time being to give Alex time to ask some questions. It wasn't as if they were in any immediate danger.

She carried on sorting spark plugs and brake blocks and cables and wheel nuts. She kept her eyes and ears open, hoping to hear something useful from Mortimer's office. He had no more calls.

⊗

Time passed. Maddie worked away in frustrated silence. Her only hope was that Mortimer would leave his office – if only for a few unguarded minutes – long enough for her to slip in there and take a look around.

Her wish was finally answered. Mortimer walked out through the open door and went over to talk to Peter the foreman. The two of them headed over to a silver Rolls Royce Park Ward.

Maddie glanced around, checking that no one was watching her. Cold fear filled her stomach. She was taking a real risk – but she had to do it.

She crouched, as though working on a low shelf. Another glance. She crept in through the open door of Mortimer's office. She kept low, her mind racing for a plausible excuse if she was found in there.

She couldn't think of one. That was bad. She would have to move quickly.

She reached up and took the telephone off the desk. She knew from what Mortimer had said that Mr L had called from his home. She sent up a silent prayer that Mr L had been speaking on a traceable land line and that the home Mortimer had spoken of wasn't the rented house in St John's Wood. She knelt on the floor with the phone in her lap. She lifted the receiver and pressed callback.

A cool female voice sounded. "You were called today at ten forty-seven a.m. The caller withheld their number."

"We'll see about that," Maddie whispered. She lifted the hem of her jeans and slipped the phone decoder out of her sock. She held it to the mouthpiece of the phone and touched a button on the side of the black box. It emitted a series of tones.

Maddie held the receiver to her ear. This time, the voice read out a phone number. Maddie recited it to herself a few times, locking it in her memory. It was not a London number.

She replaced the phone on Mortimer's desk and slid out of the office. Her heart was thumping. She'd done it. She had Mr L's home phone number. Now they would be able to get the address.

It was time to get out of there. She stood up and looked around for Alex.

He was missing.

Chapter Thirteen

Alex had had no opportunity to let Maddie know what he was doing or where he was going. He'd taken the chance that presented itself to him – he would explain later. He'd found a back exit, out of Mortimer's sight – emergency doors that could only be opened from inside. He put a spanner between the doors as they closed behind him. He hoped that no one would spot it before he got back – and that no one would notice his absence.

It was just a short jog to Chalk Farm Road. The electrics shop wasn't hard to pick out. The shop front gave a fair indication of what went on inside. The window display was a jumble of electric devices and gadgets – from toasters to reconditioned video recorders, cut-price camcorders to digital radio alarms.

Alex entered. The place was crammed with freestanding shelf units packed with electrical goods. Hand-written signs. Best Prices. We Buy And Sell. Second-Hand and New. Special Offers. If You Don't See It – Just Ask Norma. It was an obstacle course just to get through the shop.

The worn wooden counter was piled with special offers. Impossibly cheap computer software. Knocked-off videos at a quarter the usual price. Bootleg CDs.

A woman sat on a high stool, reading a tabloid.

"What can I do for you, love?" she asked Alex.

"Got any computer games?" he asked.

The woman – Norma, Alex assumed – pointed towards a cardboard box at the far end of the counter. "It's all good stuff, love," she said, watching Alex as he began to flip through the rows of plastic cases. "No rubbish."

He came to the end. Nothing!

"Is this all you've got?" he said. "I've been trying to get my hands on a copy of Nemesis 3000."

"If it isn't there, we haven't got it, love," said Norma. She frowned. "What did you say it was called?"

Alex repeated the title.

Norma's frown deepened. "It rings a bell... I remember! We did have a copy – came in a few days ago. But you're too late, love. It's gone."

"Do you know who bought it?"

A hint of suspicion entered Norma's eyes.

Alex had to act fast. He grinned at her. "It's OK," he said. "I work for Mr Mortimer." Alex loaded the final sentence with significance. "I work downstairs. You know?"

Norma looked relieved. "You had me worried there for a minute, love. You can never be too careful of people asking questions." She leant towards him. "Undercover cops. Know what I mean?"

Alex laughed. "Do you now how many police interrogators it takes to change a light bulb?" he joked.

"No – how many?"

Alex lowered his voice to a rough growl. "Shut it! I'm asking the questions!"

They both laughed.

Norma was at her ease now. "I gave the game to the boss's boy," she revealed. "Jason. He loves computer games." She winked conspiratorially. "And it never does any harm to keep in with him, does it?"

"It never does," Alex agreed. The boss? Did she mean Mortimer or Mr L?

Norma looked at him. "Why are you so keen on getting a copy, love? Is there something special about it?"

"No," said a voice from behind him. "There's nothing special about it at all."

Alex turned. Mortimer stepped out from behind a shelf unit. He must have followed him in there.

Mortimer walked slowly towards Alex. He stopped in front of him, his eyes glinting with menace.

Alex said nothing.

Mortimer broke the tense silence. "Would you like to tell me why you're nosing around here asking questions?"

⊗

Maddie couldn't understand where Alex had got to. Mortimer seemed to have gone off somewhere as well. She could see Peter's legs sticking out from under the Roller. She felt at a loss for a few moments, then she spotted the old man.

She walked over to him. "Hey – seen my friend?" she asked.

"I think he's skiving off," Kenny said with a big wink. "He'd better hope Mr Mortimer doesn't catch him."

"What are you talking about?" Maddie asked.

"I saw your pal nipping out the back way." Kenny

winked again. "He's a sharp one, though. He wedged the doors so he could get back in. He thought no one saw him." He chuckled. "But I don't miss much. I'll tell you a true story – back in the Sixties, I was running errands for Fat Frankie Fuller, and..."

"What's on the other side of the doors?" Maddie asked.

"It's an emergency exit," Kenny said. "It leads to a tunnel up to ground level." He shrugged. "Maybe he went to take a look in Norma's."

Maddie looked at him.

"Norma's?" she asked. "What's Norma's?"

⊗

Mortimer stared hard into Alex's face. "Would you like to explain what you're doing here?" he said.

Alex held steady. Keeping cool. The situation was retrievable. "I was taking a break," he said calmly. "I was told about this place. I just came over to take a look." He shrugged. "Is that a problem?"

"I told you the rules," Mortimer said. "I expect employees to ask permission before leaving the premises."

"I forgot," Alex said. "I'll remember next time, OK?" He took a step forward.

Mortimer's hand came up and struck against his

chest. "Were you thinking of going somewhere?" he asked.

"Back to work," Alex said.

"All in good time," Mortimer said. "You're a new employee, Alex, and you have to earn my trust." An edge came into Mortimer's suave voice. "How can I trust you if you won't obey even the simplest rules?" He frowned, bringing his face up close to Alex's. "Employees who don't obey the rules have to understand that there will be consequences, Alex." His eyes glittered. "If you don't shape up, you might get hurt."

Alex gazed levelly into the hard eyes. "I really don't recommend that you try that," he said, his voice soft and low.

"I see you need convincing," Mortimer said. "That's a great shame. I was hoping we could settle this amicably." He stepped back. His hand dipped into his jacket pocket. It came out holding something. A long, dark shape that fitted his palm.

Mortimer lifted his hand towards Alex. There was a sharp click. A stiletto knife blade gleamed.

Alex's stomach flipped over.

"Now then," Mortimer said, moving forwards. "Let's see if I can get you to see things from my point of view."

Deptford.

11:58.

Danny was in the MSU. His eyes were fixed on a digital clock. They were several streets away from the warehouse. He had removed the external camera and shut down all equipment. Danny didn't want to risk the MSU being detected by any counter-surveillance devices. He had to assume that an organisation like Hydra would have access to technology of a similar standard to that used by PIC. This meant that the MSU had been blind for the last two hours, a risk Danny felt they had to take. Better to back off now and risk missing something than move in too close too soon and blow the whole operation.

But now it was time.

"Let's go," he said into his face mike. "Let's do this clean. We don't want any foul-ups."

He thrust the back doors of the MSU open. Gina joined him. Together they ran across the street and along the pavement towards the warehouse.

There were three PIC vehicles on site, parked in the streets that surrounded the warehouse. Four agents to each car, one gun for each agent. Danny was in charge of the raid. He wasn't taking any chances.

At Danny's word of command, the twelve agents had made their move.

A power ram pounded into the front door. Another thumped against the back entrance.

Danny's heart was beating hard and fast. Another couple of minutes and they'd have the General and the missiles and the show would be over.

Danny listened to the noise of the attack through his headset. Crashes. Shouts. Running feet.

Then there was a strange kind of quiet.

A worm of anxiety twisted deep in Danny's guts. He had expected the General to fight back.

"Danny, you receiving me?"

"Yes, Carl. What's going on?"

"You'd better come and see for yourself." His voice sounded flat.

Danny sprinted the last few metres. He ran across the road and in through the broken-in front door of the warehouse. He made his way through to the storage space.

Most of the agents were standing there.

All eyes turned to him as he walked in.

He felt like he'd been hit between the eyes with a mallet.

The warehouse was empty.

The crates were gone.

Chapter Fourteen

Danny didn't speak for a few moments.

Someone had moved quickly – clearing the warehouse within a couple of hours.

"Looks like we've been suckered, guys," Danny said. He had difficulty keeping his voice steady. "Carl – pull in the forensic team. There won't be anything, but we should check anyway. The rest of you might as well pack up and get back to base. The party's over."

He turned and walked back the way he had come. Gina looked at him. Danny shook his head. He went into the room where he had planted the bug.

It was placed prominently on the table.

He leant over it, his hands flat on the table top, staring at it. It had been left there on purpose to taunt him.

⊗

Maddie ran along Haverstock Hill. In the distance she saw Mortimer enter a shop. She broke into a sprint, weaving in and out of pedestrians. Arriving at the shop slightly out of breath, Maddie looked inside. She couldn't see anyone. Long shelves blocked her view. Something told her to be very, very careful.

She slipped inside and edged towards the back. She could hear two voices, and as she listened more carefully she made them out – Alex and Mortimer.

Glancing around a shelf unit she saw the knife and watched as Mortimer moved forwards.

Maddie was out of cover and across the two-metre stretch of flooring in a second. Her hand chopped down on Mortimer's wrist. The knife was jarred from his grip. She dragged his arm behind his back – folding it into an unbreakable armlock. Her other arm hooked tight around his neck.

He wrenched against her but she increased the pressure. He grunted with pain and stopped struggling.

"Oi!" he snarled, his face red with rage. "What the hell do you think you're doing?"

Alex stepped forwards and picked up the knife. He crouched there, holding it across the palm of his hand. He looked up at Mortimer. The angry man was being held securely by Maddie.

"I don't want any trouble in here!" said Norma.

"There won't be any trouble," Alex said. He jammed the knife blade between two floorboards. He stood up. "You shouldn't play with knives. You might get hurt." He slammed the heel of his shoe down at an angle on the knife handle. The blade snapped off.

A muscle twitched under Mortimer's eye. "Let me go," he said quietly.

Maddie released him.

He staggered sideways, catching his breath. He smoothed his tie and straightened his jacket. His face was thunderous. "I strongly recommend that you two jokers catch the next train back to Southend. You're finished around here."

Alex smiled.

"Do we get paid for today, Mr Mortimer?" he asked.

Mortimer shook with rage. He pushed past Maddie without speaking.

"I guess not," Alex said.

The shop door slammed.

"You stupid idiots!"

They turned at the sound of Norma's voice. She was holding a heavy crowbar. "You kids don't know the grief that man can cause you. Take his advice. Get out of town – quick."

"Chill out, Norma," Alex said. "We're going."

They left the shop. Up ahead of them Mortimer was walking rapidly back towards the car dealership.

"I've got news," Maddie said.

"So have I," said Alex. "Mortimer was right about one thing – we've blown it with the car ring. Let's go somewhere quiet and swap notes. I think maybe it's time we came in out of the cold."

⊗

PIC Control.

Two hours later.

As soon as Maddie and Alex arrived at Control, they were told to report to Susan Baxendale in the Briefing Room. On their way through the open-plan offices, they heard the whisper that Danny's operation in Deptford had gone down the tubes.

They felt bad for him, but there was no time to stop now. They made their way quickly to the Briefing Room.

Danny was in there, sitting on a desk with his feet on a chair and his chin in his hands. Maddie tried to gauge Susan Baxendale's mood, but her face was as inscrutable as ever. She rested her hand briefly on Danny's shoulder in a show of solidarity. Danny lifted his head. He smiled, but she could see he was devastated by the Deptford bust. As any of them would be.

"Where's the boss?" Maddie asked Susan. Maddie had assumed Jack Cooper would be running the debrief.

"Close the door and light up," Susan said sharply. Alex clicked the door shut and flipped the switch that lit up the red conference beacon outside. Susan looked at Maddie. "He's out of the office with Agent Moon," she said. "That's all I know."

Maddie was puzzled. What could have come up in the last couple of days to send Tara and her father away? Something important, obviously.

She and Alex found seats. Alex had phoned ahead, so Susan was up to speed on developments. "We've run checks on the house in St John's Wood," she told them. "The letting agency aren't prepared to let us see their client files unless we hit them with a warrant. I sent a team over to the house, but there's been no activity so far – which makes sense if Maddie's right and Mr L is out of town."

"Have you tracked him down yet?" Maddie asked.

"We have," Susan said in her clipped, precise voice.

"The phone number you gave us belongs to a house up in Essex – in Roydon – about three kilometres outside Harlow, on the B181. You can look it up later. The man's full name is Anthony Roderick Longman. He owns and runs a Europe-wide fruit and vegetable distribution chain. He's a very successful man."

"So the car ring is just a sideline?" asked Alex.

"A highly lucrative one," Susan replied. "The cars are stolen in London and the Home Counties. They're given a makeover down in Belsize Park – and then Longman hauls them away to be sold anywhere in the UK or on the Continent, using his fleet of fruit-and-veg lorries for transport."

"Does he have a son called Jason?" Alex asked.

"Longman is married with three children," Susan replied. "Nicole – eighteen, Belinda – seventeen, and Jason, aged seven."

"So Jason *is* Longman's son," Alex confirmed.

"What's the significance?" Danny asked.

"The only thing unaccounted for from Robert Fraser's briefcase is a computer-game disk," said Alex. "It was given to Jason. If there was any information about Hydra in the briefcase – it has to be on that disk."

"What's our next move?" Maddie asked. "Close Longman down?"

"Not just yet," Susan replied.

Maddie stared at her. "What more do we need?" she asked. "We've got his name and address. We can tie him to the dealership in Belsize Park through his connections with Mortimer. We've got enough to take the car ring to pieces."

"We've got more than enough to do that," Susan agreed. "But right now, we've got something more important to deal with." Her nails tapped rapidly on her desktop. "DCS Cooper's Ministry of Defence contact believes that Fraser was involved with Hydra. So here's the story so far. Fraser used to work for Longman, but he went rogue – he took off on his own and set up in competition. At the same time, he was running armaments out of the country for Hydra." She lifted her hands, two fingers extended and touching. "Two separate careers, running parallel."

"Three, if you count his day job at the MoD," Alex added.

Susan nodded. "Mr Fraser was a busy man. Then it all started to come apart. Mortimer sent some muscle round to rough him up and to steal his car – not realising that Fraser's bosses in Hydra had already put out a hit on him."

"Because they knew he was about to be unmasked

as the UK co-ordinator," said Maddie. She remembered that from the file.

"Exactly," Susan said. "These two separate things hit Fraser on the same day. He went down. But Mortimer's thugs snatched his briefcase before the man from Hydra got to him. They don't know it, but they now have some vital information on Hydra – or so DCS Cooper's contact believes. The stolen car was taken to Belsize Park with Mortimer's briefcase in it."

"How do we know Longman isn't involved in Hydra?" Maddie asked. "He knew Fraser – and he has the means to transport the armaments out of the country."

Susan shook her head. "According to the MoD, they believed that Fraser was running the UK arm of Hydra. There was no mention of him answering to anyone else in this country. Until we get information to the contrary, we have to assume Longman knows nothing about Hydra. It seems from Danny's report of the Deptford stakeout that Hydra have pulled in a big gun – someone code-named the General. My guess is that he's been brought in from abroad to oversee the UK market. He was probably the person responsible for having Fraser killed."

"He could even be the assassin," said Danny.

Susan nodded. "Maybe so," she said. "But we have something else to focus on right now. A new target – the game disk that was given to Longman's son." Susan looked levelly at them. "We need that disk."

"So, send in the Flying Squad," Alex said. "They can pick Longman up and get the disk back off his son at the same time. No problem."

"Not an option," Susan said. "I've spoken to DCS Cooper. His orders are that no one is to move in on Longman until that games disk has been secured. PIC's priority is to get into Longman's house in Roydon, get the disk and bring it back here at top speed."

Maddie, Alex and Danny exchanged glances.

"When you say PIC," asked Danny. "You mean the three of us, right?"

"Yes."

"You want us to break into the guy's house?" Alex said.

"This is to be a top-secret operation," Susan told them. "No one outside this room is to know about it. If you're caught, I'll deny all knowledge. Danny – you will get through whatever security you find up there. Maddie and Alex – you will enter the premises and secure the disk. The operation is to take place tonight. That's all. Dismissed."

She turned to leave the room, glancing over her shoulder as she reached the door. "Alex – Maddie – I suggest you take a shower and get a change of clothes. Longman will smell you two from ten kilometres off, otherwise. And Danny? I'd like you to get this one right." The door closed sharply behind her.

The three colleagues stared after her.

"I was going to take a trip over to the Notting Hill Carnival this evening," said Danny, despondently. "I've never been – it's meant to be a total blast!" He sounded slightly dazed by the speed at which events had moved.

"We can all go over there tomorrow," Alex said. "Assuming we're not all in jail," he added, with a wry smile.

Chapter Fifteen

Danny, Maddie and Alex made use of the showers in the sleeping and recreation suite. The Supply Department loaned them some fresh clothes.

Maddie felt a whole lot better once she was clean again. The night in the abandoned flat had left her feeling like she was crawling alive. All she wanted now was to catch up on some sleep before they had to set off for Roydon. But they had agreed to meet up for a few minutes in the canteen for a bite to eat before they hit their beds.

"So," Alex asked Danny. "What went wrong in Deptford?"

"I messed up," Danny said.

"I figured that," Alex said. "Details?"

Danny sighed. "Susie B said not to risk planting any bugs in the warehouse, in case they were found."

Maddie smiled to herself – she'd like to hear Danny refer to Susan Baxendale in that way to her face. She could sell tickets to a show like that!

"So, you went in there and planted a bug," said Alex. "Against orders?"

"Yes."

"And it was found?"

"Yup."

"And they figured they'd been busted."

"Looks like it." Danny frowned. "There's one thing I don't get. Sure they would have sussed they were being watched when they found the bug – but how did they know when it would be safe for them to shift the gear? We were only out of sight of the place for just under two hours."

Maddie looked at him. "You mean, they had to know exactly what you were planning?" she said.

"I'd say so," Danny said. "I'd say that finding the bug was just the cherry on the cake." He looked uneasily at them. "I'd say those guys were watching us watching them – right from the word go."

⊗

The MSU.

North of London.

The M25/A10 interchange.

21:50.

Alex was driving. Maddie sat in the middle, Danny on the left.

They had been to Field-Ops Supply Division. In the back of the MSU was everything they would need to help them enter Longman's house undetected.

They hoped.

Nerves were beginning to bite. They drove along in silence – even Danny was subdued, or so Maddie thought. Maybe he was just feeling bad about Deptford. But if they came out of Longman's house with the disk – and if the disk held the kind of information they believed it did – then Hydra UK would be closed down. End of story.

They drove through Waltham Cross. Roydon was about twelve kilometres away.

Maddie felt slightly sick. Her mouth was dry. She wiped sweaty palms on her trousers.

Alex glanced at her. Smiling. "You OK?"

"So-so," she said. "I've never done anything like this before."

"It'll be a piece of cake," said Alex. "We've done this loads of times. Isn't that right, Danny?"

Danny nodded. "It'll be cool," he said. "No problems."

Maddie smiled and nodded. "OK," she said determinedly. "I'm ready for it!"

⊗

Roydon, Essex.

01:00.

The MSU was parked off-road under heavy trees a couple of kilometres outside Roydon. Almost hidden.

Danny stepped down from the van. He was clad in a black, skin-tight, one-piece suit. On his back was the CSK – the ultra-light Compact Surveillance Kit, an MSU in miniature. Fine leads led to a lightweight headset and to Danny's mobile communicator.

Alex and Maddie were also in black, one-piece suits. Alex was wearing a black backpack. Gloves covered their hands and masks covered their heads. Only the round disc of their faces showed. They had daubed each other's features with black camouflage paint. They were both wired up with earplug receivers and face mikes.

They climbed a fence and made their way into the trees, trying to move as silently as possible. At every crack of a dry twig, Maddie's heart leapt. She was on tenterhooks.

Danny had downloaded a military satellite picture of the house and its grounds to give them a clear overview of the target. There was the house itself, garages, some smaller buildings, a swimming pool, lawns and terraced flowerbeds, trees, a perimeter wall.

Danny paused to tap new instructions into his communicator. "This way," he said, leading them off at an angle.

A brisk walk brought them to a road. Large secluded houses were hidden behind high walls by bushes and tall trees. The road was empty of traffic and there wasn't a person in sight. Roydon seemed sound asleep.

Danny crouched by a square inspection hatch set into the tarmac.

Between them, Danny and Alex lifted it. Heavy-duty electric cables ran in and out of junction boxes.

"Keep watch," Danny said. He stretched full length in the road, his head and shoulders down the pit. He had various tools and devices to hand. He got to work.

Alex and Maddie stood over him, watching the road.

After seven minutes, Danny stood up. "OK," he said, "I've isolated Longman's house and looped in a tripper switch that I can control from the CSK. When I key in the instructions, the power goes down. You go in. You find the disk. You come out. I power her up again. No one knows a thing about it." He grinned.

They closed the inspection hatch and moved away from the road, walking in single file. Watchful and wary. Alex arrived at the sidewall of Longman's estate first. He jumped and caught the top of the wall at full stretch, levering himself up on top of it. Trees blocked his view of the house. He sat astride the wall and rested for a moment before leaning down and hauling Maddie up. She dropped down into darkness on the other side.

Her heart was hammering. The blood sang in her ears. She reached up to help Danny as he came slithering down. Alex was last.

They stood rigidly against the wall. Alex gestured for them to follow.

They huddled together under a fir tree with heavy, low branches. An ideal place from which to see and yet not be seen. There was a broad lawn, the swimming pool, the house patio doors, and a row of external security lights.

Alex touched Maddie's arm and pointed. Over to the right at the corner of the house they saw a chain-link enclosure. "Dogs," Alex whispered to Maddie. "I'll go and check them out."

She nodded. Their one-piece suits had been

specially designed for this eventuality – elastic-sealed and skintight to keep smells locked in. It made them uncomfortably hot, but the suits would help prevent the dogs picking up their scent. Of course the animals would still respond to noise and movement.

Alex crept silently and cautiously through the trees. He returned after a couple of minutes. "There's at least three of them," he whispered. "Rottweilers. They're all in the pen. If they come for us, leave them to me." He had a pepper spray. It would slow the animals down without harming them.

"Gladly," said Danny. He scanned the buildings. He pointed towards the flat roof of a garage. "I'll co-ordinate from there," he said. He handed Alex his electronic skeleton key and the black control box. "Don't break it," he said. "It's priceless."

Alex nodded, focusing on the task ahead – blotting everything else out.

Danny looked at them. "Everyone ready?" he said.

Now they had made a start, Maddie's confidence was returning. "Yes," she said.

Danny keyed in the command and pressed Enter.

In the inspection pit out in the road, a switch snapped over and all electrical power to Longman's house was cut off.

They managed to get to the house without alerting the dogs by keeping low, moving slowly and silently, stopping, listening, creeping on. Maddie was straining so hard for any sound from the dogs that it made her head swim.

Alex boosted Danny on to the garage roof, then he and Maddie slunk to the front porch. If the door was bolted, they would need to cut a window. Alex had the equipment with him: a suction disc and a diamond-point glass cutter – but that wasn't their preferred mode of entry. Too messy. He used the key, pressing the button on the battery-pack box. There were faint clicks as the key searched the internal configuration of the lock.

A minute later, Maddie and Alex were crouching in the broad front hallway of Longman's house. The pencil-thin beams of their Mini Maglites crawled the walls.

They looked at one another. So far, so good.

⊗

"We're in."

Danny heard Maddie's voice in his ears. He was stretched flat on the garage roof, his CSK at his side, his mobile communicator open in his hands. "Nice going," he whispered into the mike. On half of the screen he had an architect's schematic of the internal layout of the house. Top Elevation. Ground floor. "The two doors on your right lead into a living room," he told them. "The door on your left is some kind of reception room. The door past the stairs leads to the kitchen and dining area – I guess you can count that out for the moment."

A QWIP infrared camera was trained on the dogs' enclosure. Its array of heat-sensitive photodetectors was able to pick up energy readings up to twenty times lower than visible light. The results showed on the other half of Danny's screen. The dogs glowed white against the formless dark of the enclosure. Danny could see that all three were lying down. He hoped they were sleeping. If they started showing any signs of life, he'd know in an instant.

A PBM bionic microphone was trained on the house – shaped like a mini satellite dish, it was capable of boosting sounds by 30 decibels. Danny should be able to hear everything that went on in there.

"OK," came Maddie's whisper. "Alex is going to try the living room. I'll check out the other room."

⊗

Raymond Pallow lay on a bunk bed in a small back room of the house. He slept lightly. His knife lay unsheathed on a low table beside the bed. A door gave access to the dogs' enclosure. It was Raymond's job to keep the dogs alert and hungry. He was their trainer and their tormentor. For anyone caught in the grounds of the house, it was a toss-up which was worse – to be caught by the dogs, or to come face to face with Raymond Pallow and his knife.

Either encounter could prove fatal.

⊗

Maddie widened the beam of her flashlight and let it rove across the room. They were looking for electronics. The beam picked out a computer on a desk by the window. She padded over to it. She searched the desk for a box with the Nemesis 3000 logo. Nothing.

She found a flip-rack of disks. Thirty or more. She trained the light on them as she went through them. No games. Mostly technical and back-up disks.

All the time that she was searching, she could feel a tension between her shoulder blades – the feeling that the door would fly open at any moment and she'd be discovered.

She heard a sound behind her and as she spun round her elbow clipped a box of floppies.

They fell.

Alex stretched an arm and caught the box before it hit the floor.

Every hair on Maddie's body was on end. She could hardly breathe. "Don't creep up on me like that!"

"Sorry," he whispered. "Find anything?"

Maddie shook her head.

"Me neither," said Alex. Into the mike: "Danny?"

"Yo?"

"What's upstairs?"

"The usual. Bedrooms. Bathrooms."

"We've drawn a blank down here so far," Alex whispered. "I'm thinking maybe the kid keeps his stuff in his room."

"There are another five rooms on the ground floor," Danny said. "Give them the once-over before you start going into rooms where people are sleeping."

"Danny?" said Maddie. "Listen. I think Alex is right. I've found the family computer. There's nothing here. The disk will be in Jason's bedroom. I'd put money on it."

"Oh, great." Danny's voice was leaden.

"Head up, Danny," said Alex. "We're going for it!"

⊗

Danny fine-tuned the PBM, making sure that the angle of the dish took in the whole of the house. He could hear Alex and Maddie quite clearly as they mounted the stairs. He could hear one other sound – heavy snoring. Apart from that, the house was quiet.

He glanced at his screen. His eyes narrowed in alarm. One of the dogs was standing up, its shape shining like a radioactive ghost on the dark screen. The dog wasn't going anywhere, but it was awake now – and that was bad news. Danny decided not to tell Alex and Maddie until it became a problem.

⊗

Maddie and Alex edged along an upper corridor, their Maglite beams on narrow setting. Their eyes were getting used to the darkness and they could make out shapes. Doorways. Windows. Stairs. Pictures on the walls.

How many bedrooms had Danny said? Five?

Alex stopped at a doorway. He turned the handle carefully. Maddie stared at the crack of the door as it slowly widened. She felt more scared at that moment than she ever had.

Alex's head slid into the gap. There was a rumble of snoring. He drew back and shut the door. There was a faint click.

To Maddie it sounded like a gun going off.

Alex looked at her and shook his head. "Longman," he mouthed.

They continued along the corridor. Alex's light focused on the next door.

Maddie let her Maglite roam further. It lit up another door. On it was a small plaque with an illustration of a starship and two words.

JASON'S ROOM.

Maddie touched Alex's arm and pointed.

He smiled at her and nodded.

They crept to the door.

They had already rehearsed their next actions. Keep it simple – keep it silent – keep it quick. Alex would enter the room first. He would locate the position of the boy's bed. He would stand at the head of the bed, ready to put a hand over the boy's mouth and to restrain him as gently as possible if he woke up. Maddie would search for the disk.

Alex hoped Jason would not wake up. He wiped his hands on his suit. A sure sign of tension.

Maddie bit her lip as Alex turned the knob and pushed the door open.

The boy's bed was opposite the door.

Maddie's heart hammered.

The boy was sitting hunched up in bed, his face and chest lit by the glow of a battery-powered laptop. He was wearing headphones. He was playing a computer game in the middle of the night – with the lights out to fool his parents.

His eyes turned towards them – full of sudden alarm. His fingers halted over the keyboard.

He saw that they were not his parents and there was a moment of absolute silence. Then his mouth opened wide and he let out an ear-piercing scream.

Chapter Sixteen

Jason Longman's scream was picked up by the PBM at 95 decibels. It zapped into Danny's head like a bolt of lightning through both his ears. Stifling a cry of pain, Danny dragged his headset off. The headphones scraped on the roof. A small, sharp sound in the quiet of the night.

On the screen of Danny's communicator, the burning white head of the standing dog turned suddenly towards the garage, its ears pricked. The other two dogs lifted their heads. The first dog took a step or two forward – coming out of the enclosure through the open wire-mesh door.

Danny pressed himself flat against the roof – hardly

breathing as he stared at the screen.

The dog took another wary step forwards – then it began to bark. The other two dogs were up in an instant.

Barking furiously, the three Rottweilers loped towards the garage.

⊗

Raymond Pallow's eyes sprang open in the darkness. He reached automatically for his knife. The dogs were barking. Intruders. He hurled himself off the bed and lunged for the back door.

⊗

Maddie and Alex tumbled into Jason's bedroom. Maddie slammed the door shut and flashed her Maglite around – looking for something to jam the door. She saw a chair. She reached for it.

Alex threw himself across the room. "Danny! We need light. Power up!" he called into his mike. He reached for Jason. The boy gripped the laptop in both hands and swung it at Alex's arm. He wasn't screaming now – he was shouting, "Dad! Dad!" over and over at the top of his voice.

Maddie thrust the chair-back under the door handle and wedged it in place. That would give them a few moments' respite.

Alex was kneeling on the bed, struggling to get control over the small boy without hurting him. Bunched up in the corner of his bed, Jason hammered the laptop down on Alex's fingers.

Maddie flicked the light switch. Nothing happened. "Danny!" she said frantically into her mike. "We need light – now!"

She could hear the dogs barking. Things were unravelling fast.

⊗

Danny crawled to the edge of the garage roof. The dogs were down there, barking ferociously, jumping up at the wall with snapping jaws and wild eyes.

A man was running across the lawn. A security guard, Danny guessed. He was holding a long knife in his hand. He looked up and their eyes met for an instant before Danny scrabbled back from the roof edge. He gathered all his gear together and stuffed it into the rucksack.

The earphones lay on the roof. Through them, Danny could faintly hear a boy shouting. Alex's voice. Then Maddie – saying something about light.

"We're blown!" Danny gasped into the mike. "Get out of there!"

"Danny! We need light."

"I'm on it."

He snatched at his communicator and typed in the code to disengage the blackout switch. Lights came on. A split second later the house alarm began to shriek.

Danny crouched on the roof – trying to calculate the odds of getting to the perimeter wall before the knife-man or the dogs overtook him. Not good.

This would be a great time to call for the cavalry – except that there wasn't any cavalry. They were on their own.

⊗

The bedroom light snapped on. Alex managed to pin the boy under him. He was bitten twice before he managed to clamp his hand over the boy's mouth and get him under control.

Maddie didn't waste a second. As soon as she had light, she began to search for the Nemesis 3000 disk. The room was a mess. Clothes – books – toys – magazines – all strewn about. She picked through Jason's belongings. There was a disk box but it was the wrong one.

There were footsteps in the hall. A young woman's voice called out. A man shouted. There were thumps on the door. The handle rattled.

Maddie crouched, scrabbling through the chaos on

the floor. She saw a scattering of computer-disk boxes down at the side of the bed. Alex was sitting up with the boy pinned against him. One of Alex's legs was twisted around to lock down the boy's kicking feet, one arm holding his arms at his sides, the other hand over his mouth. Jason's eyes were wide – staring.

Maddie pounced on the Nemesis 3000 box. She flipped it open. The disk was missing. She looked at the boy. "Alex – let him speak."

Alex took his hand away from Jason's mouth. Jason stared at the door. Fists hammered and there were shouts from the other side. A man's voice – other female voices. The door rattled under the blows but the chair held firm.

"All we need is the disk from this game, Jason," Maddie said, trying to sound calm.

Jason glared at her. He struggled but Alex managed to hold him tight.

"Tell us where it is and I'll let you go," Alex panted, winded by the effort of keeping the boy pinned down.

"I threw it away," Jason said breathlessly. "It was junk. It didn't work!"

"Where did you throw it?" Maddie asked.

"Not telling! Get off me!" Jason was defiant, but Maddie saw his eyes dart towards a wastepaper bin beside his bed before he could help it. She reached for the bin and tipped it over. Rummaging quickly through the mess, she saw the disk gleaming. She plucked it out and lifted it for Alex to see.

He nodded curtly. "The window!" he said.

Maddie slipped the disk inside her suit and opened the window.

Jason renewed his struggling. He brought his head hammering back into Alex's face. The pain made Alex lose grip for a moment. Jason slipped out of his hands like a writhing snake. Tasting blood from a cut lip, Alex lunged for the boy – but he was too late.

The boy was at the door, shouting for his dad and wrestling with the chair. Alex pulled his rucksack around. He ripped out a coil of rope with a small grappling hook attached.

Maddie had got the window open. The noise of the dogs was much louder now, although from this part of the house they couldn't be seen. Alex clamped the grapple to the window frame and let the rope down.

He climbed over the sill. Their escape plan had also been thoroughly worked out. Alex to go first in case of hidden danger below. Maddie to follow.

Alex grasped the rope. He locked eyes with Maddie for a moment, then put his full weight on the rope. The grapple dug deep into the frame. Alex went hand-over-hand down the wall.

Just as Maddie straddled the windowsill, she heard a cry of pain from Jason. In his fight to get the chair out from under the door handle, he had cut himself. He held his hand out, the palm welling with blood. He stared at her – his eyes full of pain and shock.

Maddie jumped back into the room. She knew it was a crazy thing to do – but all her instincts told her to help him. She wrenched the chair away from the door so that he could get out. As soon as Jason grabbed the handle, Maddie threw herself towards the window. She stumbled over the wastepaper bin and fell. She rolled behind the bed, winded.

Moments later she heard the door burst open. Heavy footsteps thundered across the floor. Maddie tried to make herself small, huddling just out of sight at the far side of the bed. The footsteps halted at the window. A voice cursed. It was Longman. Maddie could just see his arm from her hiding place. He snatched at the grapple and pulled it loose, throwing it down out of the window.

"You won't get far!" he shouted angrily through the window. "I'll cut your heart out!"

In the background, Maddie could hear female

voices. She tried to keep as still as possible.

The heavy footsteps pounded out of the room and the voices gradually faded.

Maddie sat up dizzily. What now?

⊗

Down at the foot of the wall, Alex was waiting for Maddie to follow. She didn't. All he could see was a shadowed head and shoulders at the window. He heard a voice bellow before the grapple came hurtling down. Alex just managed to jump aside as it thudded to the grass.

Maddie was in there on her own. He had to go back for her. He ran along the wall to the corner of the house. The garages were ahead of him and he saw Danny's dark shape crouching on the roof. Raymond Pallow climbed a drainpipe as the dogs leapt and snarled below.

Running forwards, Alex drew out his pepper spray. He aimed it at the dogs as they switched targets and hurtled towards him. The first dog was caught in the face by the spray. It howled and bucked – twisting in midair to get away from the pain.

Pallow jumped down from the wall and came for Alex, drawing the knife out of his belt as he ran. Alex braced himself – crouching low, his eyes fixed on the approaching man.

The knife arm descended but Alex parried it and ducked in under the arm – landing a powerhouse blow to Pallow's stomach, then pulling the man around to act as a shield against the other two dogs.

Alex ran for the front door. Teeth snapped at his heels. He fell, losing the pepper spray. Feeling the dog on him, Alex turned on to his back and drove his forearm up between its jaws. He felt the teeth pierce the protective suit and pushed harder against the animal, forcing it back. Giving it a quick, hard chop across the muzzle with his free hand, he managed to pull loose. The dog stumbled – whining – shaking its head with shock and pain.

Alex jumped up. Something was flashing through the air towards him. He threw himself sideways as the heavy knife sliced the air less than a centimetre from his neck.

Pallow had gambled on finishing Alex with one throw but he had misjudged how quickly Alex could move – and now he was unarmed.

Alex threw himself at Pallow and the two men went rolling across the grass.

Meanwhile, Danny lowered himself off the garage roof – desperate to get down there and help Alex. But the third dog had seen the movement. It came racing back to the garage wall and sank its fangs into Danny's ankle. With a shout of pain, Danny lost his grip and fell. The huge dog was on him in an instant as he brought his arms up to protect his face.

⊗

Maddie crept along the upper hallway. All the lights were on now and the house alarm was blaring. She could hear female voices from a room at the far end of the corridor and an even louder male voice coming from downstairs. Reaching the head of the stairs, she heard a high-pitched voice yell out from behind her. She spun round to face a heavyset girl in her late teens staring at her from a doorway.

Maddie held her hands out. "Don't be scared. I won't hurt you."

The girl came at her, fists flying. Maddie backed off. A fist slammed into her cheek, snapping her head back. She had no idea how to respond to the attack. Her adversaries in training – and in life – had always been dangerous men, not frightened girls. How could she use her deadly fighting skills on someone who was only defending themselves against an intruder?

But she had to do something – the girl was unrelenting.

Maddie ducked down. The girl toppled over her,

crashing to the floor with a yell. Maddie leapt down the stairs and ran in the opposite direction to Longman's voice. Reaching the back of the house she burst into a utility room. The patio doors were locked. Another door led off to one side. There was a key rack hanging by the door. Car keys!

Maddie's eyes gleamed as she snatched the keys down. She threw the door open, finding the light switch as she ran through. She was in a big double garage. The Mercedes CL600 was waiting. Maddie opened the car door and climbed inside. It took her a moment to find the ignition. She jammed the key in and turned. Just as the engine roared into life she saw Longman in the doorway. She gunned the motor, hammering her foot down hard on the gas pedal. With a shriek of rubber the car lurched forwards. Maddie braced herself as the car rammed the garage doors. The wood splintered and cracked but the double doors did not give way. She threw the car into reverse. Longman started to move towards the car. She sped backwards and heard the bumper crack against the back wall of the garage.

Longman was at the side of the car now, trying to get hold of the door handle, shouting abuse at her, his face red and bloated with anger. She kicked forwards again, and this time the car crashed straight through the doors in an explosion of splintered wood. Peering through the woodchip-spattered windscreen, she saw Danny down by the garage wall being attacked by one of the dogs. In the rear-view mirror she saw that Longman had given up the chase. He was leaning against the shattered frame of the garage doors, clutching his chest and gasping for breath.

Maddie spun the wheel to bring the car off the driveway, pulling it around in a tight curve. She blared the horn and sent the headlight beams blazing out. The dog's eyes reflected green light as its head turned towards her. Revving the engine, she jolted the car towards the dog, which scrambled to get away.

Maddie brought the car to a halt alongside the wall. She leant across and threw the passenger door open. "Get in!" she shouted to Danny.

Dazed and bleeding, Danny threw himself into the car.

⊗

Even without his knife, Raymond Pallow was a strong street fighter. Alex fought furiously, struggling to get the upper hand. He was on the defensive – Pallow knew his job. The two dogs were circling them as they fought – barking – snarling – occasionally lunging forwards with bared teeth.

Alex was beginning to weaken from the massive body blows that Pallow was landing. No matter how hard he hit back, the man kept coming. He sidestepped a head-down rush and caught Pallow around the neck. An elbow crunched into Alex's ribs. Hands gripped his collar. He found himself hurled over Pallow's shoulder. Stunned for a moment, he lay spread-eagled on his back, gasping for breath.

Pallow loomed over Alex, sending a chill through him. Pallow had regained the knife. They had been evenly balanced before. The knife could tip the scales.

Pallow lifted his knife arm. Alex tensed, every muscle and sinew aching. He just hoped he had the strength to avoid the lunge.

Suddenly he heard the blare of a car horn. The roar of an engine. There was a swirl of light across the grass. The Merc gave Pallow a glancing blow as it skidded to a halt with a scream of brakes. Pallow twisted as he fell. The knife spun through the air.

Alex lay gasping – unable to understand what was going on. He turned his head painfully and saw the car beside him. The passenger door opened and Danny jumped out. He opened the back door. Dragging Alex to his feet, Danny pushed him into the car and jumped back in.

Maddie brought the car back to the driveway, her foot down hard. "Hang on!" she shouted, clinging to the steering wheel. The black gates loomed. She braced herself for the impact.

There was a crash and a shudder as the gates collapsed. Maddie spun the wheel with a shout of relief.

They were out!

⊗

The MSU was parked a couple of kilometres from Roydon and they were far from the main roads – hopefully hidden from pursuit. It was time to take a break and deal with their injuries.

Danny's ankle and arms were quite badly torn from the teeth and claws of the Rottweiler that had pinned him by the garage wall. Alex was bruised and battered, but he only had a few cuts. Maddie had a bad pain in her left cheek – it was tender and swollen. Longman's daughter had put a lot of weight behind that punch.

Maddie put antiseptic cream on Danny's cuts and bandaged the worst of the wounds. Fortunately none of them were deep.

Alex was speaking to Control. Susan Baxendale was on the line.

"We got it," he told her. "Mission accomplished."

"Any problems?"

"Don't ask."

"OK. Get it here fast," came Susan's cold voice. "What's your ETA?"

Alex frowned. He looked at his watch. Two a.m. "Give us an hour," he said.

"I'll expect you at two forty-five." Susan cut the line.

Alex gave a breath of laughter. "She's going to spoil us unless she cuts down on all the praise," he said.

Danny was holding the disk, staring thoughtfully at it.

"I want to know what we just risked our necks for," he said. He glanced at his colleagues. "I'm going to take a look."

He slid the disk on to his laptop. He tapped at the keyboard. A message came up on screen.

PASSWORD REQUIRED.

"Well, naturally," Danny said with a slow smile. "And I've got just the little code breaker to help me figure it out."

Alex climbed into the front of the van – trying not to show how much he ached. He started the engine. Maddie sat in the back with Danny, wondering how he intended to crack the password.

Danny drew out a metal box and wired it up to his laptop. He cracked his knuckles. "Now then, my little friend," he said, patting the box. "Let's see how quickly we can work this out."

Maddie leant back, touching her sore cheekbone. "Guys," she said, "all those other times you burgled houses – was it as hair-raising as this?"

She heard Alex chuckling. Danny was grinning.

"What's the joke?" she asked.

"We didn't exactly tell you the truth about that," Alex said. "You seemed a bit on edge – I thought you'd feel better about the op if I said we'd done it before."

Maddie stared from Alex to Danny. "You lied?"

"Yup," Danny said, still concentrating on his laptop.

"Have you ever done anything like that before?" she asked.

"No," said Alex. "This was our first time." He laughed. "I think it went pretty well, all things considered."

Chapter Seventeen

Danny's flat in Bloomsbury, WC1.

Bank Holiday Monday.

03:35.

The room was lit only by the computer screen.

Danny's attempts to discover what was on the Nemesis 3000 disk had been only partially successful. His box of tricks had managed to crack the password within twenty-three minutes, while the MSU had still been making its way through North London. But then he'd hit a wall.

The disk was encoded. Danny could do nothing to read the gibberish that appeared on screen, so he had cut his losses and copied the entire file on to his hard drive as it was. Now that he was at home, he had time to do some more work on it. He stared once again at the password. BROKEN ARROW.

He instructed the file to open. The screen changed. A mass of incomprehensible symbols scrolled out. Danny tried a few commands, but nothing happened. Throwing himself back in his chair, he felt briefly at a loss as to what to do next. He was determined to get into that file – even if it took him all night.

⊗

Maddie was sitting cross-legged on her bed, watching her portable TV. She was too wired-up to sleep. Although her body was crying out for rest, her brain wouldn't switch off. She was watching a news item on the first day of the Notting Hill Carnival on BBC News 24. Children's Day. It looked wonderful. Fun. A great day out – if you didn't happen to be working every waking moment for Susan Baxendale.

Maddie's head began to drop. Heavy eyes. Brain getting fuzzy around the edges. She reached for the remote. Another item caught her attention.

"Extraordinary new facts have emerged concerning the shooting of top civil servant, Robert Fraser," the newsreader was saying.

Maddie rubbed her eyes and tried to concentrate.

"The Ministry of Defence has just issued this brief statement to the press."

Maddie was fully awake now. Christina Brookmier had certainly wasted no time in getting the news out – they had only handed the disk over to Susan Baxendale an hour ago!

The scene changed to a press office, where a middle-aged woman was sitting behind a long table. She had dark hair, pulled back off a sharp-featured, pale face.

"First of all," Christina said, "I'd like to thank you all for your patience and your endurance in staying up so late for this briefing."

She began to read from a prepared document. "A rigorous internal investigation by the DPA has revealed that Robert Fraser had been leading a double life for some years. He abused his role as a Senior Advisor to the DPA executive board to aid his criminal activities. Suspicion began to focus on Mr Fraser several weeks ago, but while evidence was still being gathered, it is believed that he became aware of the investigation. He may have been preparing to flee the country when he was shot."

The report cut back to the newsreader in the studio.

"Ms Brookmier went on to say that Mr Fraser's death is believed to have been the result of a dispute within the criminal organisation with which he was involved. The investigating team uncovered vital new evidence, which made it clear that Mr Fraser was at the head of a criminal chain that has been responsible for putting many millions of pounds worth of illegally exported arms into the hands of terrorist organisations. Ministry of Defence sources say that with the death of Mr Fraser and the discovery of this new evidence, they will shortly be in a position to dismantle the UK arm of this organisation."

"Yesss!" Danny punched the air in triumph. It had taken a while to cover all the options, but he had eventually discovered that the file had been encrypted by an augmented 'PGP' system – and once he had that piece of information to hand, it had only taken him a few minutes to grasp the basics of the cryptographic code and to translate the whole thing.

It had been worth the trouble. The disk was loaded with information about Hydra's UK operation: drop zones, dead-letter offices, smuggling routes by air and by sea. Border control bypass protocols. Maps. Schedules of meetings both in the UK and abroad. A long list of contacts and their code names. A complete itinerary of items smuggled, going back two years.

It made for scary reading. These people had been putting some seriously nasty weapons into terrorist hands.

And judging by a diary file it looked as though Fraser had been the lynchpin of the British end of the organisation for several years.

"He was in the right job for that line of business," Danny muttered as he opened file after file – revealing more and more information. "Instead of buying weapons and then handing them over to the army, he was selling them to any bunch of thugs that could afford them." He frowned. "You were a seriously bad man, Mr Fraser."

⊗

Maddie switched the TV off and slid into bed. She lay sleepless in her darkened bedroom, hands behind her head, her eyes open. A couple of things about Christina Brookmier's statement were playing on her mind. Maddie understood the nature of PIC well enough to realise that no one in the organisation wanted its work splashed all over the television, but it bothered her that Brookmier had made it sound as if investigators in her own department had discovered the new evidence that put Fraser's guilt beyond doubt.

Maddie's face ached, Danny had been chewed up and spat out by a Rottweiler and Alex had been a punchbag for one of Longman's thugs – all this and they hadn't even warranted a mention. Even a comment such as 'we had invaluable help from...' would have been fair. It was frustrating to hear Brookmier making it sound like she'd masterminded the whole operation.

The other thing that puzzled Maddie was the speed with which Brookmier must have had the disk decrypted. OK, Danny had already solved the password puzzle for her, but that still left her with the problem of actually being able to read the nonsense that came up on screen. The disk had been decrypted and read and a statement had been prepared for the press – all within the space of sixty minutes. Someone on her team must be a real computer wizard.

⊗

Bloomsbury.

04:00.

Something about that file was bugging Danny. He could see why it would be necessary to keep certain information – codes and contact names and detailed accounts of on-going operations, but why had Fraser kept so much old data? Arms smuggling was risky business – a person would be crazy to keep one byte of info on file after it was necessary, but Fraser seemed to have kept everything over a two-year period. It didn't make sense.

And that wasn't all. Previous armaments shipments were documented in fine detail – where the weapons came from, how they were transported, code names of contacts all along the route, their final destination, prices of each item and details of how the money was handed over.

And yet there was no mention of those twenty crates of Starstreak missiles that Danny had discovered in the Deptford warehouse. Sure, the file might not be up to date, but it must have taken some pretty complicated logistics to get the missiles to Deptford – and that must have taken weeks to organise. So why no mention of it?

He began to explore the files on the disk more thoroughly, unsure what he was looking for. He opened a utility software programme called EMSCOPE. It had been designed to help recover 'lost' files and to retrieve information from sectors no longer highlighted by the current file index pointer. He had upgraded it with some ideas of his own. It was now possible to pull deleted fragments of files up from a whole series of disk sectors and to reassemble them to create a contiguous unedited file. The result was like a virtual 3D X-ray of the file – revealing the various layers of deleted information hidden under the final product.

Danny hunched over his computer keyboard, tapping at the keys – watching the results as they were displayed on screen. He punched in the final command and sat back. A whole series of deletions were highlighted and revealed. The excitement of the moment raised goose flesh on Danny's arms. The file had been totally rewritten. He stared at the screen in disbelief. This was dynamite!

Jumping to his feet he ran his fingers through his hair. He stretched, keeping his eyes pinned to the amazing stuff that his investigations had thrown up. He went into the bathroom, splashed some water on his face and checked his watch.

It was four thirty-seven. Time to make a phone call.

⊗

Alex awoke to his telephone ringing. Surely he couldn't be late – wasn't it Bank Holiday? He threw an arm out and grabbed the receiver. "This had better be good," he mumbled sleepily into the phone.

"Alex – it's Danny – and it's very good."

Alex sat up, reaching to switch on a light.

"I've been working on the disk, Alex." Danny's voice was hushed and urgent. "You're not going to believe what I've found. Fraser was just a fall guy. He had nothing to do with Hydra UK. The General runs the whole thing – and always has done. And I'm standing here looking at the General's real name right now."

"Who is he?" asked Alex.

"No. Listen – I don't want to do this over the phone," Danny said, his voice suddenly filling with unease. "This is too big. I don't know who might be listening. Meet me in the Pret A Manger café in Notting Hill Gate at eight o'clock."

"I'll be there," said Alex. "You be careful, Danny."

"Will do."

Alex lay back in his bed. Danny had sounded excited but nervous. And whatever he had discovered, it had made him fearful that someone might be tapping his phone.

Alex understood why Danny had chosen Notting Hill as a meeting place. Up to two million people would be attending the Carnival later that day – what better way to hide than in such a huge crowd? But the question that robbed Alex of sleep was – why did Danny feel he needed to hide at all?

What was so special about this?

Two men were hunched over surveillance equipment in a small room while a third, shadowed figure guarded the closed door.

A snatch of recorded conversation was being replayed.

Meet me in the Pret A Manger café in Notting Hill Gate at eight o'clock.

"We need to do something about him, General," said one of the seated men. "We should act now."

The General nodded assent. "Enter his flat," the General said in a menacing whisper. "Destroy his computer and bring me any disks he's been working on." There was a brief silence before the General spoke again. "Oh – and eliminate him for me – make it look like a domestic accident."

Danny was exhausted. He collapsed fully clothed on to his bed. He needed a few hours of sleep before meeting up with Alex. His sleep was shallow and fitful.

He was awoken by a faint, sharp noise. His eyes snapped open as he listened intently, hardly breathing.

The sound came again. A click from the front part of his flat. Danny knew that sound – it was the noise that an electronic key made just before it opened a lock.

Danny bounded off his bed and ran light-footed to

the door. He opened it a fraction and peered out into the darkened hallway. He could just make out the front door in the gloom, and it was beginning to open.

Carefully he closed his bedroom door and turned the key in the lock. "Stupid!" he berated himself. "You don't have the brains you were born with. They were bugging your phone, Danny." He took a few deep breaths, trying to calm himself. He heard the faint creak of someone moving along the corridor. "OK," he whispered. "Now, this is scary."

Someone knew what he had discovered. And now they were coming for the evidence – and for him. His computer was in the living room. The proof of his findings was out of reach.

There was one good thing – his father was away on business. Danny was alone in the flat.

Licking dry lips with a dry tongue, he listened at his door, but all he could hear was silence. A bad kind of silence.

The door handle began to turn very slowly. That was it. Enough. He was getting out.

Danny opened the window and stared down at the ground four metres below him. He climbed through the window and perched on the sill. Breathing deeply, he checked over his shoulder into the room. He hoped that the intruders hadn't left lookouts outside.

He turned and slid off the sill, supporting himself on his arms as he lowered himself down the wall. His shoes scrabbled at the bricks. Gritting his teeth, he brought himself down to hang full stretch from the windowsill.

He let go.

Chapter Eighteen

The morning was already warm as Maddie sat at the kitchen table, eating the scrambled eggs on toast that her gran had prepared for her, watching more news on the TV. Gran was out on the balcony, pruning and deadheading her pot plants.

"Lovely weather for the Carnival," she remarked to Maddie. "Are you going?"

"Yes. I thought I'd give Laura a call," said Maddie. "Maybe round up a few people and make a party of it." Maddie smiled. "Do you want to join us, Gran? It'll be great."

Her gran laughed. "Too noisy for me!" she called

back. "Too many people."

Maddie was about to switch to a music channel when an item of breaking news hit the screen.

"An Essex businessman was arrested at his Roydon home in a dawn raid by officers of the Serious Crime Group. Anthony Longman, who owns and runs an international food distribution company, has been linked to a London-based criminal organisation specialising in the theft and resale of luxury motorcars across Europe. More arrests are expected soon. Our crime reporter, Penny Wilde, is in Roydon now."

The scene shifted to an outside broadcast unit where a young woman was addressing the camera. Behind her Maddie recognised the remains of the black iron gates of Longman's home. There were dark skid marks on the tarmac and the lawn was ripped to shreds.

It was strange to think that she had made those marks only a few hours ago – and now she was sitting at her own table, drinking orange juice and seeing the scene of their late-night operation on breakfast television. The place seemed a lot less threatening in daylight. Penny Wilde reported that Longman was being held in a London police station and that the rest of his family were behind locked doors and were refusing to give interviews.

Maddie hoped they had locked Raymond up as well. It would only be a matter of time now before Mortimer and his associates were in the bag. Operation Hubcap had been a complete success.

The phone rang and she picked up. It was Alex.

"Have you been watching the news about Longman's arrest?" she asked him.

"Yes." His voice was oddly subdued. "Listen, Maddie, I know this is meant to be a day off – but there's something going on – I thought you might want in on it."

Maddie listened with growing curiosity as Alex told her about Danny's phone call.

"I tried calling him a while ago," Alex said. "There was no answer."

"Are you worried?" Maddie asked.

"No. Not yet. I'm due to meet him at Pret in Notting Hill in half an hour."

"I'll be there," Maddie said without hesitation.

"Great. Maddie? Danny seemed pretty nervous – keep your eyes open, OK?"

"What am I looking for?"

"I don't know – anything out of the ordinary."

⊗

Anything out of the ordinary. Alex had to be kidding! Maddie negotiated her Vespa down Queensway and made a right into Bayswater. She was still some distance from the main route of the Carnival, but already the roads were clogged.

The excitement and anticipation of Carnival was growing. Some people were already in costume – laughing and calling to one another and blowing whistles. From several streets away, Maddie could hear road crews checking their sound systems.

Maddie parked her scooter in a side street off Notting Hill Gate and made her way through the crowds towards Pret A Manger. The glass and chrome-fronted café was busy.

Squinting against the bright, early-morning sunlight, Maddie spotted Alex. He was on a stool at one of the high tables, drinking coffee. She made her way over to him. He had bought her a cappuccino.

It was five past eight, but there was no sign of Danny.

"I've been trying his number all morning," Alex said, pressing speed-dial on his mobile. He held it to his ear. "Nothing," he said. "It's not even switched on."

"Maybe he went out without it," Maddie offered.

"Danny?" said Alex. "Without his mobile? I don't think so."

"We should call Control," Maddie said. "He might have contacted them."

"Who might have contacted them?" asked a deep voice. They turned.

A curious figure stood behind them, dressed in top hat and tails made from scarlet crushed velvet and covered all over in sparkling red sequins. Similarly decorated gloves covered his hands. Even his shirt and shoes and socks were bright red. His face was completely hidden behind a grinning cat mask.

It was Danny.

"Danny – you're OK," breathed Maddie.

He leant close to them. "I'm not so sure," he said, slipping the mask down. His eyes moved around the café. "In fact, I've got a bad feeling that I'm a whole world away from OK."

"What happened?" Alex asked.

"After I called you, I decided I could use some sleep," Danny said, keeping his voice low. "Then I heard someone in the flat. I managed to get out through the window. I hid out for a while. Some guy was prowling around looking for me. Another guy joined up with him and the two of them went off in a black car. I left it an hour or so, then I crept back to my place to see what they'd done." Another nervous glance around. "They'd poured acid or something all over my computer. It was just a big heap of melted junk. All my disks, too." He grimaced. "They made a very thorough job of it."

"Who were they?" Maddie asked.

"Good question," Danny said. He brought his voice down to little more than a whisper – Maddie could hardly hear him over the other conversations in the café.

"Like I told Alex, I spent the night decrypting that disk," Danny said. "Most of the information in those files is fake. All the contact names – the drop-zones – the code words – all faked. I found a whole bunch of deleted stuff. But here's the killer – when I did some digging, I found out that Robert Fraser's name had been used to overwrite another name right through the file."

"Anyone we know?" Alex asked.

Danny nodded. "The person codenamed the General is Christina Brookmier."

Maddie stared at him. "My dad's contact in the MoD," she breathed.

Danny nodded. "You got it – and, according to the disk, she runs Hydra UK." His eyes widened. "I'm pretty sure she's found out that I know about it. Which makes me public enemy number one."

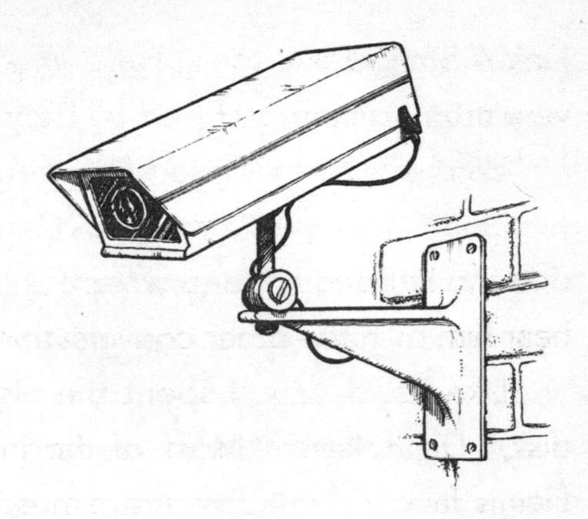

Chapter Nineteen

A black Vauxhall Zafira with tinted windows was parked at the southern corner of Pembridge Gardens, W2. A man sat in the back. He was watching Pret A Manger through Swarovski BP 10 x 25 mini binoculars.

Traffic and pedestrians frequently obstructed his view across the road, but every now and then he got a clear sight of the three young people seated huddled together at the table in there.

"Do we take them?" asked the driver.

"No, not yet," said the man in the back. "They're all prime targets now – it's just a matter of time."

Pret A Manger.

Maddie still felt stunned by Danny's revelation.

"You have to tell Susan about Brookmier," she told him.

Alex nodded. "Control can put out an All Points Bulletin on her – track her down before she gets to you."

Danny looked at them, his face deadly serious. "All the evidence is in a lump of melted-down plastic back at my flat," he said. "Do you think she's going to take my word for it?"

Maddie was surprised at this. "Of course she will," she said.

Danny looked at her. "Your father and Brookmier go way back, right?" he asked.

Maddie nodded. "They've known each other for years."

"Does he trust her?"

Maddie opened her mouth to reply – but shut it again without speaking. She realised what Danny was getting at. It was his word against Brookmier's. No one at Control would think he was lying about the disk, but without corroborating evidence, they might think he'd got it wrong.

"Susie B is already mad at me over the Deptford

business," Danny said. "If I'm going to take this to her, I'll need some hard facts."

"We need them fast," Alex said. "Brookmier is a smart woman – she'll have started making plans the moment she found out you'd cracked the disk."

"She's been watching us all along the line," Danny said. "I knew there was something screwy about the way they cleaned out the warehouse. We've been taken for suckers."

Maddie was trying to get a grip on what had been happening. "Her own investigation must have been getting too close to the truth," she said. "So she planted the faked disk in Fraser's briefcase – and then she had him killed. When they investigated the murder, the police were meant to find the disk and decode it."

"She gave it a password and encrypted it, so it would look genuine," Danny added. "I bet she freaked when she found out the briefcase was missing."

"The police sealed off Fraser's house and office," said Alex. "So there was no way for her to plant another copy of the disk. She had to get the original one back, otherwise the plan to frame Fraser wouldn't work. And when the disk was stolen, she needed someone she could trust to find it for her. That's when PIC came into the picture."

"And just to be on the safe side, she kept tabs on us throughout," Danny said. "We were supposed to hand the disk over to the police. They'd crack the password and decrypt it – and bingo! They'd find the fake evidence. Case closed. And she'd carry on as boss of Hydra UK as if nothing had happened. I guess she never figured anyone would think to look at what was under the surface of that disk."

"So what do we do?" Maddie asked. She would have gone straight to her father with this – but she had no idea where he was, and the only way to contact him would be through Susan Baxendale – which led them right back to Danny's credibility problem.

"There is one way forward," Alex said. "But it's not going to be easy. Danny's evidence has been trashed, so the only other way of getting to the truth is via Brookmier herself."

"Oh – cute idea," said Danny. "I'll go ask her. Oh, and I'd like white lilies at my funeral, please."

"Alex is right," Maddie said. "We have to convince her to meet us."

A fire lit in Danny's eyes. "Got it!" he said. "I'll call her and tell her I've got another copy of the disk. I'll tell her I'm prepared to trade with her and that I'll give her the disk and keep my mouth shut – for a couple of hundred thousand pounds in cash."

"She'll think it's a trap," Maddie said.

"Probably," Alex said. "But she'll still need to meet with Danny – to find out for certain whether a second copy of the disk exists."

"We need a fast way of contacting her," Danny said. "A phone number."

"There'll be a personal contact number in the file," Maddie said. "I'll go to Control and get it."

"While you're there," Alex said. "There are a couple of other things you could pick up. A wire – so we can get her on tape – and a bullet proof vest." He glanced at Danny. "In case things turn bad."

⊗

PIC Control.

09:43.

The lift doors hissed open and Maddie stepped out into the main office. Normally, by this time on a Monday morning, the place would be humming. But on this Bank Holiday Monday there was only a skeleton staff on duty. Jackie Saunders, the Communications Officer, was at her desk.

Maddie smiled at her.

Jackie Saunders frowned. "Aren't you due a day or two off?" she asked.

"I'm not here to work," Maddie said lightly. "I'm just picking a few things up and then I'm out of here."

"Going to the Carnival?"

"You bet."

Maddie made her way through the room to her own work station. She booted up her computer. The office was strangely quiet. All but two of the wall-mounted monitor screens were blank. There was hardly any sound from the desktop servers and printers. She could hear very clearly the sound of one person tapping at a keyboard on the other side of the room.

She brought the Hydra file up on screen. She scrolled rapidly, hunting for a contact number for Christina Brookmier. She found it: office, home and mobile. She scribbled the numbers down, exited the file and closed down her computer.

She waved goodbye to Jackie Saunders as she went past. She stepped into the lift and pressed for the Supply Department two floors down.

It wouldn't take her more than a couple of minutes to get what she wanted – and then she'd be gone. With any luck, her subsequent explanation for her unscheduled visit to Control would come complete with a taped confession from Christine Brookmier.

⊗

Avondale Park, W11.

12:41.

It was half a kilometre from the heart of the Carnival, but even at that distance Maddie, Alex and Danny could hear the rumble of bass-heavy music.

Danny had left his own phone at his flat. He borrowed Alex's to make the call to Christina Brookmier's mobile number.

He heard a ringing tone.

Maddie and Alex were watching him closely. This had to be good. Danny grinned at them – cool as ice. He didn't want them to know how he was feeling inside.

"Brookmier." A crisp, alto voice.

"Hi, there," Danny said. "I think we need to talk, General."

"Who is this?"

"Take a wild guess," Danny said. "I'm just some guy who's good with computers." He allowed a sarcastic tone to enter his voice. "Are you getting warm, yet?"

"Ahh. Mr Bell."

"Y'see – it wasn't that hard to figure out after all, was it?"

"What can I do for you?"

"It's more a case of what I can do for you, General,"

Danny said. "Let me paint you a picture – I'm standing here and I'm holding a shiny new CD-R in my hand. It's a copy of something I was working on last night. Can you guess what's on the disk, General?"

"What do you want?"

"Straight to the point," said Danny – super-cool. "I like that. Here's the deal, General. We meet, OK? You bring half a million pounds in cash and I hand over the disk and promise to keep my mouth shut. Do we have a deal?"

There was silence down the phone. Alex and Maddie looked at Danny.

"How do I know you haven't made more copies?" Brookmier asked.

"I guess you'll just have to trust me," Danny replied.

"It will take me several days to get the money."

"No way!" Danny shouted into the phone. "We do this today or I go show the CD to my boss. Do you think I'm dumb enough to let your goons track me down and pop a bullet in my brain?"

"Calm down, Mr Bell. No one needs to get hurt."

"Newsflash, lady!" said Danny firmly. "People have already been hurt. You think I don't know what happened to Robert Fraser? No way am I going down like that. I want you off my back, OK? Let's get this over with. You need that disk – I want the money. End of story. Now – do we have a deal or what?"

"We have a deal."

"Good. Here's the plan. We meet at three p.m. today. There's a building on the north side of Elgin Crescent – on the corner of Kensington Park Road. The first floor is a launderette – above it is a place that makes Carnival novelties. There's a black door by the side of the Launderette. It'll be unlocked. Take the stairs up to a door that leads you out on to the roof of the next building along. There's a metal stairway up to the roof. I'll be waiting for you up there. Come alone or I'm gone."

"Elgin Crescent?" said Brookmier. "That's on the Carnival route, I believe. Maybe I should wear something appropriate."

"Wear what you like, lady – just bring the money." Danny cut the line and let out a breath. "How'd I do?" he asked.

"Oscar-winning performance, Danny," Maddie said.

Alex nodded. "That was the easy part," he said. "Now let's get back to the Carnival and lose ourselves in the crowd until it's time for the meet." He gave Danny a long look.

Danny raised his eyebrows. "Problem?"

"You understand that she'll want to kill you?" said Alex.

Danny nodded without speaking. He understood that only too well.

Chapter Twenty

Montpelier Square, Knightsbridge.

An elegant, spacious drawing room.

Elgar's Enigma Variations was playing softly on the Bang & Olufson hi-fi system. There was a Sanderson-weave carpet on the floor. In the bay window a perfectly ordinary man sat at a desk that was covered by a green baize sheet. On the sheet lay an antique pocket chronometer, made by Charles Nephew & Co of London and Calcutta in 1869. It had a silver Hunter case. A white dial with Roman numerals. The hands were blued steel.

The man was leaning close. In his fingers was a

watchmaker's screwdriver – a precision instrument that he had taken from a small wooden box with a sliding lid. He watched through a jeweller's eyeglass as he made fine adjustments to the delicate inner workings of the chronometer.

The watch had been losing almost five seconds a day and the man could not stand disorder. Towards the back of the desk an open laptop pinged as a message appeared.

YOU HAVE MAIL.

The man frowned, opening the mail. He read it and typed a reply, which he sent.

His new assignment was in Elgin Crescent, Notting Hill. Three p.m.

Three targets this time – three times the fee. Excellent. He glanced across at his Shreveport grandfather clock. Twenty-five past one.

There was ample time to finish this job before he had to pick up his silver briefcase and go to Notting Hill.

He resumed the work on his pocket watch as if nothing had happened.

⊗

The black Zafira was parked in Walmer Road, W11.

The man with the Swarovski binoculars watched the three figures leave Avondale Park and cross the road into Hippodrome Place. "They're heading back towards the Carnival," he said. "Get as close as you can – then you'll have to follow them on foot." His eyes glittered. "Don't lose them."

The driver turned the key in the ignition and the Zafira glided smoothly along the road, like a panther stalking its prey.

Maddie, Alex and Danny joined the crowds that lined Ladbroke Grove. It was a warm, sunny day. The Carnival parade filled the street with a kaleidoscope of colour and motion. A sound system blasted out the Sly and Robbie remix of Black Uhuru's 'What is Life?' – perfect carnival music, with a bass line that rocked the pavement and made Maddie's ears ring.

Stalls lined the streets selling exotic foods and Afro-Caribbean arts and crafts.

Maddie bought Alex and Danny some highly-spiced Jamaican patties: saltfish and ackee. They made their way deeper into the heart of the Carnival. Steel bands competed for audiences on opposite corners. There were more sound systems, some of them with up to two-dozen speakers, pouring out an endless stream of music. Soca and calypso rhythms mingled with reggae – acid jazz and soul melted into hip-hop – funk and house clashed with garage.

There were people from a huge range of ethnic backgrounds – a great melting pot of people all drawn together by the excitement and the thrill of the largest street Carnival in the whole of Europe.

People milled around – many of them in costume – some of them blowing shrill whistles – some of them dancing in the streets. All of them having a great time.

Maddie found it impossible not to be affected by the atmosphere that swirled around her and for a few minutes she almost forgot why they were there.

Almost.

Danny seemed determined to enjoy himself. He joined in with a street-corner band, hammering away on a borrowed Surdo drum as the infectious samba rhythm set people dancing. Maddie found herself dancing with the others, briefly losing herself in the rush of the moment.

Only Alex kept himself aloof, his eyes piercing the crowd, his mind focused on the task ahead. He had come to a decision. He was wondering how Danny would take it.

They made their way slowly through to Powis Square, where live sound stages had been set up. More music. More noise. More dancing.

Alex looked at his watch. It was half past two. Time to go.

⊗

The parade route stretched down the length of Ladbroke Grove. It turned left, winding its way southwards until it met Westbourne Grove. Then it headed north up Chepstow Road – Great Western Road – Kensal Road – back to its starting point. A great five-kilometre loop.

Huge, colourful floats glided slowly along the crowded streets. People paraded, dressed as fantastically coloured birds and butterflies or clad in abstract costumes that exploded with colour and light. But the three PIC agents had no time to enjoy the parade. They had work to do.

⊗

All the preparations for the meet with Brookmier had already been made.

Before Danny had made the call, Alex had spoken with the woman who ran the Launderette on the corner of Elgin Crescent. The upper floors of the building were closed for the holiday. She had a key. Alex had shown his PIC pass. She had handed the key over. Alex had scouted the place out. It was his decision that Danny should meet with Christine Brookmier on the rooftop. A private oasis in a public place. The flat roof wouldn't offer any cover for uninvited guests.

The three of them edged their way through the crowds. A huge float glided past, all flowing red and green silk, shaped like a dragon, pouring out the unmistakeable muscular rhythms of the Japanese Kodo drummers.

Alex closed the black door, reducing the noise.

They walked up the stairs in single file.

Alex first, then Danny, with Maddie at the rear, glancing back every now and then to make sure they weren't being trailed. They came to the floor where a door led to the adjacent roof. They went into a side room. Maddie took the bulletproof vest out of her bag whilst Alex made sure the mike on the wire was working.

Danny was unbuttoning his shirt – preparing to have the wire taped to his chest.

"What will you do if she has a gun?" Alex asked.

"Stick my hands in the air," Danny quipped. "Look, I'll be wearing the vest. It's cool. I can handle it."

Alex's eyes narrowed. "I should do it," he said.

Danny frowned. "You think?"

Alex nodded. "I'm quicker and stronger than you – and I've got a black belt in karate. If anything goes wrong up there I'll handle it better than you. You know I'm right."

"You're white – I'm black – I think she'll notice the difference, Alex," Danny reminded him.

"I'll be wearing the cat mask," Alex said. "The top hat will hide my hair. By the time she notices I'm not you, we should have enough on tape to put her away."

Danny's forehead creased. "I don't know..."

"Alex is right," Maddie said. She smiled at him. "You're the brains of the group – Alex is the brawn."

"I wouldn't have put it quite like that," Alex said with a half-smile.

Danny looked at him uncertainly.

"Do you want to arm wrestle for it?" Alex said.

Danny shook his head. He carried on unbuttoning his scarlet shirt. "You'd better not get killed up there, Alex," he said. "If you do, I'm never going to trust you again."

Chapter Twenty-One

The south corner of Elgin Crescent and Kensington Park Road.

A white stone, neo-classical building.

14:55.

Christine Brookmier stood to the side of a second-storey window. She knew she was taking a risk by being here. Better by far to pull the strings from a distance. That had always been her rule. That was why she had survived for so long. But she needed to be certain that her orders were carried out to the letter.

She looked down into the street below. Her eyes filled with contempt for the excited crowds. She had seen the three PIC agents go in through the black door. If the assassin fulfilled his contract, none of them would come out alive.

She looked at her watch.

It was almost three p.m. Another few minutes and it would be over.

It had been a gamble to use PIC, but an unavoidable one. The disk had to be recovered and Jack Cooper's hand-picked team had the training and the resources to find it. But she had underestimated them. They had been more thorough in their investigations than she had expected. She should never have used a genuine Hydra disk to try to frame Fraser. She should have opened entirely new files rather than overwrite old ones. But it had never occurred to her that anyone would dig deep enough to discover the changes she had made. It had been an error – but an error that would shortly be put right.

The corner house opposite had four storeys – the building next to it, only three. A red iron stairway led from one rooftop up to the other.

Brookmier shrank back from the window. She saw a movement from the lower roof. A single figure dressed in scarlet top hat and tails. There was a mask over the face.

She felt a sense of satisfaction and relief as she watched Mr Bell climb the steps and walk across the roof towards his death.

⊗

"OK," Alex murmured. "I'm on the roof. There's a chimney stack right across the centre." He looked over his shoulder. "There's access to the roof from other buildings. She may not come your way – but keep out of sight just in case. If you hear anything, give me the word. I'm going to take a look around up here."

"Be careful." Maddie's voice was an anxious whisper in his ear.

Alex smiled. He was always careful.

He paced across the roof. The broad, brick-built chimney stack was a couple of metres high. It would make good cover if things got out of hand.

He positioned the cat mask more comfortably over his face. He'd be glad to finish this. The red-sequinned suit was stifling him and the mask made it difficult to see properly.

He came around the stack.

He halted in his tracks. Below him, Maddie and Danny heard the sharp catch of his breath.

"What is it, Alex?" Maddie asked.

Alex didn't reply. He had company.

A figure stood at the edge of the roof – facing towards the street – leaning slightly forwards, one foot up on the low parapet. It wore a long dark cloak. A cowl covered the head. It seemed to be staring down at the Carnival procession.

Alex stepped into the open. He didn't speak or move. The figure straightened up and turned towards him. A skeleton mask covered the hooded face. Brookmier had said she might wear something appropriate for Carnival.

"Should I be scared?" Alex asked.

In the room beneath Alex's feet, Maddie and Danny stared at one another. There was someone already up there.

The figure lifted a hand to its face and drew the skull mask away. It wasn't Brookmier. It was a man.

A pistol emerged from the folds of the cloak. "Hello, Alex," said the man. "I've been looking forward to seeing you again."

⊗

Maddie and Danny huddled close to the receiver. They could only just hear the rooftop voices above the clamour of the Carnival parade.

"Where's Brookmier?" they heard Alex ask. "This wasn't the deal."

"My client sends her apologies, Alex," said the other voice. "But you people haven't kept your part of the deal either. Wasn't Danny meant to be coming up here to do the exchange?"

"How does he know us?" Maddie whispered to Danny.

Danny shook his head.

"Did you bring the money?" Alex asked.

"You know there isn't any money, Alex," said the man. "You knew what was going to happen up here. That's why you came instead of your friend. Very noble of you." The man's voice was calm and reasonable. "I take it the other two are in the building – listening to everything we say. Maddie – Danny – I have a gun – if you don't come up here immediately, Alex will be shot." He looked at him. "You seem a little bulkier around the chest than last time I saw you. A bulletproof vest, maybe? Haven't you read the files on me? One clean shot in the head and the job is done."

Alex frantically searched his memory. Who was this man? How did he know them?

Maddie stared up at the ceiling. She was sure that the threat was genuine. They had to go up there. They couldn't leave Alex to die. She turned towards the door. Danny caught her by the wrist. She looked at him. He shook his head.

"We stay right here," Danny said, staring into her eyes.

Alex's voice sounded again over the receiver. "Am I supposed to be impressed that you know our names?" he asked.

"You haven't worked out who I am yet, have you, Alex?" said the other voice. "Let me jog your memory. Now – what can I tell you? We never actually met face to face, but we came close. I was watching you through a telescopic rifle sight. You were wearing a white shirt. You were talking on a mobile phone. I actually had you in my sights at one point. You weren't my main target, but I was prepared to kill you if you became a threat to my safety. But then I got the abort message."

With a sickening jolt, Maddie suddenly realised who the man was.

The truth hit Alex at the same moment.

"Spider!" he hissed.

His mind flashed back a few short months.

The Wimbledon Lawn Tennis Championships. Centre Court. The Men's Final. A young British player, Will Anderson, had received death threats. PIC had been there to protect him. Spider had been contracted to assassinate him. Alex had spotted the muzzle of Spider's rifle. He had raced to intercept but the assassin had gone – the hit had been called off at the last moment. Spider had left his mobile phone. There had been a text message: HELLO ALEX. NEXT TIME YOU'RE DEAD.

"You do remember me," Spider said. "How kind." He lifted the gun and aimed it at head height. "I don't think your friends are coming. Sorry, Alex. Goodbye."

He squeezed the trigger.

The single, loud crack of gunfire hit Maddie like a physical blow. There was a cry of pain. Maddie grabbed Danny's arm, her whole body shaking. She stared up towards the roof. She could hardly breathe from the shock of what had happened.

Alex had been shot.

Chapter Twenty-Two

Pain seared through Alex's shoulder as he sprang forwards and to one side. Had he hesitated for a split second longer, the bullet would have finished him. He had known his only chance of surviving up there would be to make that desperate lunge for Spider's gun. The impact of the bullet had knocked him sideways – blunting the force of his attack. He was vaguely aware – through a red mist of pain – that Spider was lining up for a second shot.

He curled into a tight forward roll, feeling the hot asphalt under his back. He kicked out hard with both legs. His feet slammed into Spider's body. Spider stumbled backwards. His calves hit against the low brick parapet.

Terror contorted his face as he fought for balance on the roof edge. Alex instinctively tried to reach out for him. He watched helplessly as Spider's arms windmilled. Their eyes locked for a moment as the assassin toppled backwards off the roof and disappeared – the cloak billowing around him as he fell.

⊗

Brookmier saw the assassin fall, crashing down on to a flower-covered float. She heard screaming. She saw panic erupt in the crowd.

But her heart was cold. His death meant nothing to her. He had failed her – that was the one thought that consumed her now. Jack Cooper's brats were still alive – still a danger to her. She had to escape. She turned from the window and found herself staring into the clear green eyes of Tara Moon.

⊗

Danny sprang up at the sound of the gunshot. "Stay put," he said to Maddie. "Call for backup." He ran to the door and was gone.

Maddie could hear noises coming through the receiver. The sound of heavy movement. A distorted crackling and rumbling. Alex gasping for breath. Hope rose in Maddie. He wasn't dead – not yet. She dreaded the sound of more gunfire.

Call for backup!

She reached for her mobile.

Alex's phone chimed. It was lying on the floor – left aside when Alex and Danny had swapped clothes.

She snatched it up.

"Alex – it's Jack Cooper."

"Dad?" Maddie gasped.

"Maddie? Listen – this is urgent. Tell Alex to get to the white building opposite. I sent Tara in there to arrest Christina Brookmier but I've lost contact with her. I think she's in trouble."

Maddie's mind reeled. "Alex has been shot!" she gasped.

"Understood. Sit tight, Maddie. I'll get help."

The line was broken.

Maddie ran to the window. She could hear screams and shouts from the street but she had no time to think about that. She quickly located the white building on the other corner.

Alex had Danny to help him. Tara was alone – she needed Maddie's help.

Maddie threw herself across the room and took the stairs in threes. She came crashing out into the street.

Maddie put her head down and ploughed through the chaos of jostling bodies. She reached the building gasping. It had black railings and steps leading up to a large black doorway. The door was half-open. Maddie ran into a broad, high-ceilinged hallway. She could hear nothing above the roar of the crowd and the thumping rhythm of carnival music.

She ran for the wide staircase, acting on instinct. She came to a halt on the landing. The upper corridor ran in both directions. There were several doorways. She looked around but could see only more stairs, more rooms.

She was baffled by the size of the building. Tara and Brookmier could be anywhere!

A figure appeared at the head of the upper staircase. It was Brookmier.

⊗

In an upstairs room, Tara Moon lay clenched in a foetal position, unconscious. It would be fifteen minutes before the effects would begin to wear off. She had been taken out by a single shot from an M18 Advanced Taser. The weapon looked like a gun, but it fired two hooked probes – propelled at forty metres a second by compressed air – able to strike down a target at up to five metres distance. On contact, the probes sent out

26-watt electromagnetic disruption impulses – scrambling the victim's nervous system – locking the muscles and causing total shut down.

⊗

Maddie's breath hissed.

Brookmier was staring down at Maddie, gripping something in her right hand. She raised her arm and took aim. Maddie froze. It was a gun.

Brookmier began slowly to descend the stairs. Maddie was a clear target. There was nowhere to run, nowhere to hide.

Brookmier was halfway down the stairs now – only a few metres from Maddie. Her face was blank, but a deadly light burnt in her eyes.

Maddie stared at the gun. But was it a gun? It was gun-shaped, but it seemed to be made of black plastic. It was certainly like no gun that Maddie had ever seen. She made a snap decision.

Maddie sprang towards the staircase – convinced that the gun was a fake – unaware of her peril. Christina Brookmier pointed the Taser and fired.

⊗

Danny hit the roof running. Careless of his own safety, he sprinted around the stack – his mind was focused entirely on getting to Alex.

He came to a stumbling halt. Alex was lying against the parapet, one hand clutching his shoulder. Blood darkened the arm of the scarlet jacket. He was alone.

Danny crouched at Alex's side. Alex looked up at him, his face tight with pain. "He went over the side," he said. "I couldn't do anything."

"Forget him," Danny said. "C'mon – we need to get you to a doctor."

⊗

Maddie's attack seemed to have taken Christina Brookmier by surprise. She fired the Taser without any apparent aim.

The two probes snaked past Maddie's head and embedded themselves in the far wall of the landing. She saw the hair-thin electric wires stretching taut above her shoulder. There was a hissing crackle as the Taser emptied its charge into the plasterwork.

Now Maddie understood what she was up against – and how close she had come to being disabled by Brookmier's hi-tech weapon.

She flung herself at the woman – using all her weight and force to body-check her and bring her down on the stairs. She gripped Brookmier's wrist, holding her arm away as Brookmier fought to bring the EMD terminals into contact with Maddie's body.

Brookmier was strong. As hard as Maddie struggled to keep her arm locked back, Brookmier was still managing to bring the Taser closer and closer to Maddie's face.

Anger surged up through Maddie. This woman was a traitor! She had sold weapons to terrorists. She was responsible for the deaths of countless people and had organised the assassination of Robert Fraser. It had been her fault that Alex had been shot.

With a furious shout Maddie twisted her hand around and Brookmier's arm suddenly buckled at the elbow. The end of the Taser touched Brookmier's neck and Maddie tightened her finger on the trigger.

The weapon discharged. Maddie sprang back. Brookmier convulsed on the stairs for a few horrible moments and then became still.

Maddie fell to her knees. It was over.

A phalanx of police officers cleared a way through the crowds that surrounded the yellow float. A few of the officers climbed up on to its back. Hundreds of sunflowers had been fixed on to a huge dome-shaped frame. The impact of the falling body had caved the dome in. One of the officers pushed her way in through the wall of yellow.

The damage inside the dome was severe. The vault of slender wooden struts was smashed and broken. Wire supports had been stove in. Broken flower heads and petals were scattered about.

The officer fought her way out into the open again. Her colleagues looked at her expectantly. She stared down at her Sergeant, shaking her head – baffled. "There's no one in there, Sarge," she called down, against the roar of the music. "Not a trace. Whoever it was – they've gone."

⊗

The black Vauxhall Zafira raced along St Quintin Avenue, W10. PIC Agent Gina Sidiropoulos was at the wheel. In the back were DCS Jack Cooper and Maddie. They were heading for Hammersmith hospital.

Two ambulances had gone on ahead. Danny was with Alex in the first. Alex's wound was serious but not life-threatening. He had been lucky. The bullet had passed right through his shoulder without hitting bone. Paramedics had quickly controlled the bleeding. He just needed patching up.

Tara Moon had regained consciousness within a quarter of an hour of being hit by the Taser blast. She had looked bad. Jack Cooper had insisted that she be checked over by doctors. She was in the second ambulance with Christina Brookmier and two police officers. Brookmier was also awake – handcuffed to an officer – head down – weak and nauseous. Her life as the General was over.

Maddie was trying to process a lot of new information.

"I was suspicious of Chris Brookmier from the start," said Jack Cooper. "I've been in the police for thirty-five years and I've developed an instinct for when people are spinning me a line. I arranged a private meeting with the Secretary of State for Defence. He agreed to give me full access to all the documentation on the Defence Procurement Agency's internal investigation – including Chris's personal, password-protected files."

Maddie raised her eyebrows in surprise.

"That was when things started to get interesting," Jack Cooper continued. "Chris's private files showed that she had learnt all about Fraser's links with the underworld. But she had suppressed the information – she had her own plans for him."

"Fraser must have seemed like a godsend," Maddie said. "The perfect person to put in the frame as the head of Hydra UK when the investigation started to get too close to her."

"Exactly," said her father. "I went to the Home

Secretary and asked for a phone tap. Chris was monitoring PIC's every move – the only way I could keep tabs on her was by disappearing myself. I knew she was watching Danny in Deptford but I had to let her make her move. If I'd warned him, she'd have known she was under surveillance."

"Did she know about our trip to Roydon?" Maddie asked.

Her father nodded. "She knew everything about it," he said. "Including the fact that Danny copied the disk." He narrowed his eyes at the memory. "Chris was very busy that night. She picked up the disk at Control and then went straight to the news briefing at St Anne's Gate." He laughed softly. "I think she wanted to make sure she got the news out before PIC. She obviously doesn't understand how we work."

Maddie knew what he meant – her father would never have briefed the press on the operation. PIC couldn't do its job in the glare of the media.

"That explains how she managed to make that statement so quickly," Maddie said. "She didn't have to decrypt the disk – she knew exactly what was on it."

"After the press briefing, she went to Bloomsbury," said her father. "She'd set up a surveillance team to watch Danny. That was a dangerous time for him. I sent

Tara to make sure he was alright but he managed to get out of the flat on his own, so Tara didn't show herself. I guessed the three of you were cooking something up – so we've been keeping tabs on you."

Maddie frowned. "How did you know where we were?" she asked.

Her father smiled. "Remember the mobile phone I gave you when you went undercover?" he said. "It had a tracker bug in it."

Maddie stared at him.

"Just a little insurance, Maddie," her father said. "I hate being taken by surprise."

⊗

Hammersmith hospital.

17:25.

Alex was sitting up in bed. His shoulder was heavily bandaged, but he was awake and reasonably alert.

Maddie sat to one side of the bed, Danny to the other. Maddie was exhausted – surviving on raw nerve ends. Ready to crash out at any moment. But she had been determined to fill them in on all that she had learnt in the drive over there with her father.

Danny also had some news.

"Tara's been allowed to go home," he told her. "She's fine, they say. And Brookmier has been arrested and taken into custody. I saw her as they took her away – she looked sick."

"Good," Maddie said. "I hope she gets what's coming to her."

"I think that's a given," said Alex. "She must have caused a lot of misery over the years."

Danny smiled. "We won, guys," he said.

Alex's eyes smouldered. "Except that Spider got away," he said grimly.

"We wrecked his reputation for never failing," Maddie said. "He was supposed to kill us – and we're all still alive."

Alex relaxed back into his pillows.

"Do you think Spider's the kind of guy who would come back to finish the job?" he asked.

Alex smiled tiredly. "If he does, I'll just have to throw him off another roof," he said.

"Let him try it," Maddie said. "We're a match for him."

Danny grinned. "The three of us – we're a match for anyone."

Maddie smiled. But she wasn't so sure. She had a bad feeling that they hadn't heard the last of Spider.